Crazy in Love

Crazy in Love

Dandi Daley Mackall

DUTTON CHILDREN'S BOOKS

DUTTON CHILDREN'S BOOKS
A division of Penguin Young Readers Group

Published by the Penguin Group
Penguin Group (USA) Inc., 375 Hudson Street, New York, New York 10014, U.S.A.
Penguin Group (Canada), 90 Eglinton Avenue East, Suite 700, Toronto, Ontario, Canada M4P 2Y3 (a division of Pearson Penguin Canada Inc.) • Penguin Books Ltd, 80 Strand, London WC2R 0RL, England • Penguin Ireland, 25 St Stephen's Green, Dublin 2, Ireland (a division of Penguin Books Ltd) • Penguin Group (Australia), 250 Camberwell Road, Camberwell, Victoria 3124, Australia (a division of Pearson Australia Group Pty Ltd) • Penguin Books India Pvt Ltd, 11 Community Centre, Panchsheel Park, New Delhi - 110 017, India
Penguin Group (NZ), Cnr Airborne and Rosedale Roads, Albany, Auckland 1310, New Zealand (a division of Pearson New Zealand Ltd) • Penguin Books (South Africa) (Pty) Ltd, 24 Sturdee Avenue, Rosebank, Johannesburg 2196, South Africa • Penguin Books Ltd, Registered Offices: 80 Strand, London WC2R 0RL, England

CIP Data is available

Published in the United States by Dutton Children's Books,
a division of Penguin Young Readers Group
345 Hudson Street, New York, New York 10014
www.penguin.com/youngreaders

Designed by Beth Herzog

Printed in USA First Edition

ISBN 978-0-525-47780-8

1 3 5 7 9 10 8 6 4 2

To Jen and Dave, who are also "Crazy in Love"

ACKNOWLEDGMENTS

I want to thank my wonderful editor, Maureen Sullivan, who has just the right editorial touch. Thanks for seeing the promise of this story and for helping me get it there. I'm very glad you are one of the voices in my head.

Thanks to Dutton Children's Books, with whom I'm "crazy in love."

Table of Contents

1

The Rents

Okay, so I do hear voices in my head, but they're all mine. And before you go dialing Psychiatrists-R-Us, consider the fact that I'm going to need all the help I can get just to have a fingers-crossed, fighting chance of getting through today.

My senior year was not supposed to start out like this. Not after the best summer ever, hanging with my gal pals and dreaming about being totally free next year when we'd all sail away to college but keep in touch with each other and still be us forever and always: The Girls.

I admit that I had my doubts about the greatness of the summer when Alicia, my all-time best friend, left early for college. But Cassie and Jessica and I visited nine college campuses, including fraternity rows and mixed dorms, even though Cassie and I had already settled on Illinois State University. We exhausted every possible joke connected with the fact that our university is located in *Normal,* Illinois, which means we'll be meeting Normal guys and dabbling in Normal nightlife, and having Normal love affairs.

On other long summer days Cassie and I met up with Jessica and Samantha to sun at Jessica's pool because, cancer or no cancer, tan fat looks better than white fat. On occasion, Nicole and Star and Company would meet us at the mall. We'd hook up with some of the guys and see a crummy summer movie half a dozen times just to make fun of it or drive up to Six Flags Great America and flirt shamelessly with Bugs and Daffy and try to get them to fight over us.

So how did I get from that all-American summer to this soap-opera-worthy mess?

"Mary Jane!" Mom yells up the stairs like a normal person would yell only in the event of a life-threatening fire. "Your *fah*-ther and I need to talk with you."

Mom only calls Dad my "*fah*-ther" when she wants to conjure up images of 1950s head-of-the-household, better-be-real-scared-of-me men. Although she also calls my *fah*-ther "Tom," "Thomas," "your dad," and "Daddy," according the need of the moment, she has only one name for me, her younger daughter.

Mary Jane. Like the shoes, which I wouldn't wear if they were the last foot-covering on a desert island.

I told you the voices in my head are mine. But I blame my mother for encouraging ***Plain Jane*** to take up residence in my head. Like the shoes that bear my name, ***Plain Jane*** is not so much plain as timeless, classic, loved by mothers everywhere, a good investment, a good bet, a good buy . . . and *so* not fun.

I try very hard not to listen to her.

"Now, Mary Jane!" screams my mother.

"Coming, Mom!" I shout, reaching for my red lipstick. But then I hear ***Plain Jane*** in my head, reminding me that my mother hates red lipstick and says it makes me look like one of those street people, and she's not talking about mimes.

In spite of myself, I put down the Flame Red tube and apply wholesome lip gloss to my lips. I have nice lips, if I do say so myself. Very kissable, says ***M.J.*** (another voice in my crowded head, a voice that can only be described as sexy). ***Plain Jane***, on the other hand, hates my lips. She says they do not go with my eyes, which are small and brown and ordinary, the eye color of three-quarters of the earth's inhabitants. ***Plain Jane*** never misses an opportunity to point out my plainness, and she adds that I should simply be thankful for the good vision provided by my plain eyes. ***M.J.*** counters that these eyes are intense, sexy even.

Before Mom can shout again, I dash from the bathroom back to my bedroom and grab my pack, in case I need to make a fast getaway.

I think about sliding down the banister, but ***Plain Jane***'s voice is shouting that normal people do not slide down banisters, and I go with her voice, since this battle is with the rents. They love ***Plain Jane***.

They're in the kitchen, sitting together at the table. If my parents belonged to someone else, I'd probably think they were nice-looking, for middle-aged rents. Dad has all of his hair, which is brown and matches his eyes. And mine. And three-quarters of the known world's. The fact that he isn't balding is a point of pride for him, since his younger brother, my Uncle Jim, has just about lost all his hair. Dad's in pretty good shape for a lawyer. And he doesn't have the stereotypical lawyer personality. He doesn't even hate lawyer jokes, although I'm not always sure he *gets* them.

Mom is small, five feet two, to Dad's six-two, with me taking the middle at five-eight. She's blonde, blue-eyed, and bubbly, in a sincere way. If they have ugly secret lives, I don't know about them yet. But I'm only seventeen.

"Have a seat, Mary Jane," Dad says. Even now, when I know he's been up all night obsessing about me, his voice is warm, like a radio announcer's before the game.

I sit. As always, Mom has set the table for breakfast, even though I skip it half the time because I'm running late. I pour Grape-Nuts into my bowl, hoping to ease the tension with the appearance of normality and healthy bits of grain.

Mom obviously can't take the waiting anymore. "Mary Jane," she begins, and her disappointment is so thick in only those two words that, in spite of myself, I feel guilty. I know this disappointment. It's like a second skin to me, a fur coat in the dead of summer.

Throughout my colorful past, the ***Plain Jane*** in my head has arranged my rents' disappointment into words of various patterns: *"After all they've done for you, how can you do this to them?" "Why can't you think of someone besides yourself?" "You owe them everything, and all they ask is that you live by their rules. What is wrong with you?"*

Mom glances at Dad to get the okay. Gets it. Goes on. "Honey, we heard you come in last night."

"Sorry," I say, before thinking enough. "I tried to be quiet. I didn't mean to wake you." This is what the ***M.J.*** in my head was saying, and I knew better than to listen to her.

"You know good and well that's not the point," Dad says, his voice firmer now. He and ***M.J.*** are seldom on the same side. They know how to push each other's buttons. "Let's not play games, okay? I thought we'd gotten over this phase."

"Sorry," I say, pouring the milk and trying hard to tune out the smart aleck in my head. "I know. It was late."

"One a.m.," Mom helpfully supplies.

"School-night curfew is still ten unless you check with us first," Dad reminds me. "Your mother and I were very worried about you."

"I called," I offer. "Did you get the message?"

"We called, too," Mom says. "Your cell was off."

M.J. is whispering a dozen excuses to me, just like that. She's so good. *You called my cell? Really? I have to remember to plug in that phone every night*. Or, *Are you sure you called the right number? I didn't get a message.* Or, *One of the kids I was with needed to call her parents, and they talked forever.*

I'm smart enough to pass on the ***M.J.*** excuses just now. "That was stupid of me," I admit. "I should have known you'd try to call back. I turned off my cell because we were trying to watch the end of the movie. I'm sorry. I just didn't think."

"That's the problem, Mary Jane. You haven't been thinking," Dad agrees. "One o'clock on a school night? You've been working hard all these years to get into a good school like ISU. Don't lose it your senior year. College isn't—"

"I thought you were studying at Cassandra's house," Mom interrupts. "That's what you told me."

"I was!" I protest. "We're having a quiz in English on *Julius Caesar* today. We were watching the Shakespeare production. That's what we were doing. It's a really long movie. We just didn't get it started in time."

All truth. Nothing but the truth.

Not the whole truth.

The movie was running, but we didn't do much watching. Unless you count watching each other. I spent most of the time watching Jackson House. Six-foot senior, long brown hair, killer smile. Star Simons's boyfriend. The ***M.J.*** in my head firmly believes that anyone named Star Simons doesn't deserve a boyfriend like Jackson House. And it's not just the name. Star would be the first one to tell you Jackson belongs to her. But that doesn't stop her from sneaking in dates with other guys. I have this on reliable authority.

And there's more. There's a sadness in those big brown

eyes of Jackson House. I've seen it. It's kept me awake nights. And I can make him laugh! Which turns befriending him into a kind of community service, when you think about it. And I do. Think about it. Constantly.

"Mary Jane?"

"Sorry. Thinking about the exam."

"There's still no excuse for being out that late," Dad continues. "You shouldn't wait until the last minute to study. The habits you form now are the habits you'll carry with you to ISU." His voice is already softening, and so are his eyes. He is so easy. It's enough to make the ***Plain Jane*** in me say, *Shame on you.*

"You're right, Daddy." And he is. Still, I don't think I'm going to get grounded. I almost never do, thanks to ***Plain Jane***, who is highly trustworthy. I don't think Dad's even going to yell at me. I can't imagine what Alicia's parents would do to her if she'd gotten home that late. Alicia is probably my best friend in the whole world, but I would never trade rents with her for five minutes.

I turn to Mom, who looks like she has a lot more to say on the subject. If I give her time, she's going to ask who was there (fourteen of us) and where Cassie's parents were (Kansas City or Des Moines, I think) and if I bothered to read the play before watching it on television (no). "I'm sorry I worried you, Mom. It won't happen again."

"I hope not," she answers, her voice filled with hurt. And, yes, disappointment.

I gulp down a few bites of cereal.

"Don't forget your sister's game after school," Dad says.

"I won't," I answer, although I *had* forgotten about Sandy's game.

M.J. is singsonging in my head: *Yes! Not even a grounding! I win! I win!*

But as I grab my pack and walk out of the kitchen, I have to admit that I feel a little guilty. It's only 7:37 a.m., and already I've disappointed my rents, forgotten about my sister's big game, and gotten myself a monster-truck-sized crush on somebody else's boyfriend.

2

The Girls

I back Fred down the driveway. I refuse to use car mirrors, despite the warnings from my old driver's ed instructor about the dangers of looking over one's shoulder. So my head is turned backward while I inch onto Elm, gravel crunching as if I'm breaking it. How could turning around to back out be less safe than backing by mirrors? Side mirrors lie. They even admit it in tiny white letters that warn: OBJECTS IN MIRROR MAY BE CLOSER THAN THEY APPEAR. How can you trust a mirror like that? It's like thinking you're skinny because you're in front of the right mirror in the funhouse.

Fred is my Dodge Neon, bright blue, circa 1997. I love Fred. Dad turned it over to me when he got the Blazer.

Turned it over to you FREE and even paid your insurance, you ungrateful, ugly American, ***Plain Jane*** is quick to add.

It takes me about ten minutes to make the drive to Attila High, also known as Attila Ill here in Attila, Illinois. The sun's still trying to find a spot in the gray sky where it can pop out. November in Illinois is no April in Paris.

I use the time to prepare myself for what I know will be waiting for me at school. Cassie, for sure. Jessica, Samantha, Nicole, Lauren. The Girls have probably been heating up the airwaves with cell phone energy, pooling information and observations about last night. They will not like what they undoubtedly see as a potentially dangerous development in the peaceful coexistence of our group.

A family tree diagram of The Girls would show two major branches. There's the simple branch with Cassie, Jessica, Samantha, and me. And then there's the slightly twisted branch with Star at the tip, supported by Nicole and Lauren. This twisted branch shoves its way to the top of the tree as it fights for a position above all other branches. To the casual observer, The Girls are one big happy family tree, with leaves connecting all branches and providing group shade. But from the inside, The Girls are all too aware of the delicate system of interlocking branches, the swaying and creaking of those branches in the wind.

The Girls will not like this perceived threat to the tranquility of the tree. They will not like it, but they will love talking about it.

For the millionth time, I wish Alicia hadn't graduated ahead of me. Alicia Freedman is my true best friend. But now she's off in another world at Southern Illinois University, with college and fraternity guys. And I'm back here, trying to survive high school . . . with all these high schoolers.

This morning, it will be up to me to say the right things that will preserve all remaining high school female friendships still available to me. I will have to convince The Girls that of course I would never do anything to hurt one of The Girls. And I wouldn't. Of course. I was not, absolutely not, making a play for Star's boyfriend, even though I know he's unhappy with Star, who has never been known for her faithfulness to any boy. Even though said boyfriend does smell like the forest after a rain and is the only human worthy of the cliché about "eyes that twinkle."

No. None of this matters. I would never do anything to upset The Girls. So surely all will be well.

I park Fred, and The Girls are on me before I switch off the ignition.

"Hi, guys!" I call, as they back away enough to let me out of the car. I lock it and face them. I'm going for a look that says, "What's going on? Did I miss something? Duh."

It's just three-on-one at the moment. Cassie, Jessica, and Samantha against me. All part of the *good* branch.

Cassie is the first to speak, probably because her home was the scene of the crime. "We wanted to . . . well, we thought you ought to know. People are talking, Mary Jane."

I frown. Think deer caught in the headlights meets Snow White. "Talking? About what?" I sling my backpack over one shoulder and start heading in to school.

Jessica elbows Cassie, who says, "About Jackson. It's all over school."

"Huh?"

"Seriously," Cassie continues. "I mean, Star's *got* to know."

"Okay," I say, doing my best to maintain the Snow White deer look, which isn't easy because ***Plain Jane*** is calling me a slut. Never mind the fact that the only time Jackson and I touched was when our hands met under fluffy white puffs of corn in the popcorn bowl. "Star's got to know what?"

Lauren and Nicole are coming toward us, and the odds have just slipped to five against one.

"Hey, Lauren! Hi, Nicole!" I wave.

They don't.

Nicole is the big deal in Thespians. She's had the lead in every play since first grade. Right now, she could be auditioning for *Gone With the Wind,* the part where somebody breaks the news to Scarlett that the Civil War thing is out of hand.

"We have to talk, Mary Jane!" Nicole exclaims. She glances both ways, as if crossing a street, although we're all on the sidewalk. I suspect she's making sure she has an audience.

"We've just been with Star," Lauren adds.

Someone gasps. I think it's Samantha.

"Star?" I glance from friend to friend.

"She was crying," Nicole whispers.

The Girls emit sympathetic *ahs*.

So do I. I think I'm drawn in by Nicole's acting ability.

Nicole shakes her head and sighs deeply, empathetically, dramatically.

"Star's crying?" I ask. But I don't believe it—not for one minute. Star Simons shedding tears? In kindergarten, she thought *Bambi* was funny, and that includes the big-bang scene with the offstage deer mom. I've seen Star remain unmoved when everybody else in fifth grade cried their heads off because our class pet, Ginny the Guinea, got loose and ate Mars, Venus, and Pluto from Jenny Strand's Styrofoam science project and died right in the middle of our classroom, her little guinea pig legs all pointing to the ceiling fan.

"Wait a minute. You're not trying to tell me that Star's crying because of me?" I ask, clarifying things. "Or because of something I've done? No way!"

Nicole is obviously Star's direct ambassador. "The guys, well, some of them, the ones who were at Cassie's with us last night, I guess they've been all over how you and Jackson . . ."

"Jackson?" I'm offended. "And *me*? Who said anything about Jackson and *me*?"

"I know *we* didn't say anything," Jessica offers, glancing at the others for nods of assent.

"There's nothing to say!" I insist. "I can't believe anybody would even think about Jackson and me in the same thought."

The ***Plain Jane*** inside my head reminds me that I have

thought of little else for the past twelve hours, that I purposely and traitorously got up early and spent extra time on my hair this morning in case I happened to bump into Jackson in the hall. She calls me *disloyal* for fixing my hair and adds that it doesn't look that great anyway.

I try again. "I would never hurt Star. Doesn't she know that? Jackson and I were just goofing around."

"She's really upset," Nicole says, not letting go of her ambassador mission.

"You guys *were* pretty chummy," Jessica offers.

"You really did look like you were talking," Samantha agrees.

M.J. is screaming in my head, *Excuse me? Did I miss the part where Star and Jackson got engaged?*

"Plus," Nicole begins, glancing away, as if searching the audience for answers, "Star knows about you and Jackson leaving the party together."

"Leaving together?" My voice cracks. "To get more pop? You've got to be kidding me!" I turn to Cassie. "You were all about me going out to get more pop, Cassie!"

She shrugs, noncommittal, apparently waiting to see how all this shakes down.

"Fred was practically the only car there!" I remind them. "We had popcorn and no pop! Okay, no diet. And you can't count ginger ale. Unless you're desperate. Or hurling. Somebody had to go."

"And somebody named Jackson had to go along for the ride?" Lauren mutters.

"He volunteered!" I protest. "Nobody else did. Massive pop is heavy, in case you haven't noticed."

The truth is, I was so nervous being in Fred alone with Jackson that I couldn't have taken advantage of the situation if I'd wanted to. We drove to Fast Gas two blocks from Cassie's house, bought pop, and I drove us back. I think we talked about the weather, although I did make him laugh once.

Nicole takes it upon herself to set out the facts of the case for the jury. "I'm just saying that Star knows you and Jackson left the party together . . . and came back together."

"After four minutes!" I cry. "With diet pop!"

Plain Jane has stopped calling me *slut* and is now whispering that I should just calm down and assure my friends that this whole discussion is simply too silly for words. I'm not pretty enough to be anybody's girlfriend, much less Jackson House's.

And suddenly, I don't know who to believe. ***Plain Jane*** or ***M.J.***? Nicole and Lauren or me? I don't know what to think. Or what's really real. What if I am actually turning into a boyfriend thief? That is so not me! I am and always have been loyal and true to The Girls.

"Help me, you guys!" I sniff with total sincerity. The tears that are making my friends blurry are real. "I can't stand having you guys think I did something wrong. I can't take it if you're all mad at me."

"Oh, Mary Jane, we're not mad at you!" Cassie gives me a hug. She's an inch shorter than I am, with too-blonde hair that can change faster than a chameleon. When she hugs me, all seven of her stairstepped silver earrings cut into my chin. Thank heavens she's wearing a coat, or who knows what damage her belly rings could cause.

"Promise? You believe me, don't you?" I ask. "Because I really didn't mean anything. You know me. I was just horsing around."

"The guys are calling it flirting," Nicole relays.

"Flirting? I wasn't flirting! Why would they say that? Why would those guys try to start trouble? Why would they make something up about Jackson and me? I feel so horrible that Star bought into this trash. I feel like it's my fault."

Jessica and Samantha have joined in the group hug. Nicole and Lauren stay where they are, apparently firmly in the Star camp.

"You didn't do anything," Jessica says. She lets go, backing out of the hug, and I can see she's crying, too, which makes me cry more, which . . .

Girls. You gotta love us.

"Hey," Cassie says, wiping her eyes with the flared sleeve of her vintage black velvet jacket, "how much trouble did you get in when you got home last night?"

"Enough," I answer, shooting her a pitiful look designed to enhance the sympathy factor. Parent–friend dynamics can be pretty tricky, so I say no more. It is never cool to be grounded when you're a senior in high school. But it's also uncool *not* to be grounded when you do something grounding-worthy. Being trusted by the rents creates suspicion.

"My parents didn't even wake up when I got in," Samantha informs us.

"Thank goodness for late-night martini habits, huh?" Cassie says.

"Well." Nicole is on the wrong side of the odds now—two to four. But she and Lauren are standing strong, unmoved, ambassadors to the Star. "I can't be late to Spanish again," Nicole says, turning to go. Lauren follows suit.

"Nicole!" I shout after them. She turns. "Tell Star I'm sorry if something I did upset her. Okay?"

She nods, but it's more like a chin jerk. No smile. The kind of thing you'd do if someone gave you a left uppercut.

This is not over.

Yet as I walk into Attila Ill, my girlfriends surround me. We are comrades. We are one.

I am grateful.

But the day is young. And as we step inside the crowded, noisy halls of Attila Ill, ***M.J.*** is already murmuring, *Now where is that major hottie? Jackson House, here I come!*

3

Betrayal

We Girls split for our lockers, then dash to first-hour English. Half the class was at Cassie's last night. The sleepy-looking half. At least I won't be the only one to crash and burn on this test. What is it about Shakespeare that makes him so test-worthy?

Mr. Schram frowns as I skid in just under the bell. The man was born to be an English teacher. He looks like those old English kings in PBS movies, the seriously obese fellows, who graze from long wooden tables piled high with barely cooked pigs and enormous turkey legs they fling over their shoulders after devouring. His too-small tweed jacket, a souvenir of better days, has no chance of camouflaging his tremendous belly.

The entire Attila Ill football team couldn't apply enough power to button one button on that jacket.

"Cutting it close, aren't we, ladies?" he observes, as Samantha and I step over outstretched legs to get to the empty seats.

"Sorry," says Samantha, snatching the first empty chair.

I am not looking for Jackson House, although I can smell him and sense his presence. Plus, I know where he usually sits. I have blinders on as I slide through his territory, third row, third seat, and take a seat in the far back corner, where no one, not even Ambassador Nicole, can accuse me of flirting.

I am being watched. I sense this without looking around. Observed. And not just by our English teacher.

I risk a bored glance to the front of the room and can see Nicole out of the corner of my eye. She's turned around in her front-row desk so she can keep an eye on me. I'm starting not to like that girl.

I long to gaze over at Jackson. What if I caught him looking at me? What if our gazes met?

"I hope you've all been studying your Shakespeare," Mr. Schram warns. "*Julius Caesar,* to be exact."

"The Shake!" Jonathan Anderson cries, fist raised in salute. I went to homecoming with him our sophomore year.

Jonathan Anderson, ***Plain Jane*** muses. *As I recall, he dumped you for Melissa Charbon because she had breasts.*

Ah, the ever-insightful ***Plain Jane.***

But it's ***M.J.*** who gets in the last word on the subject of Jonathan Anderson: *You could get Johnny back if you wanted* *to, wrestle him right away from Theresa Magill, his current girlfriend. But Jonathan Anderson is no Jackson House.*

I pull out my English book, hoping that I'll magically spot quiz answers as I flip through the play. I heard enough of the plot in the background last night to know bad characters plotted against good characters. At least one person got killed. Somehow I don't think these are the kinds of details Schram will be looking for. All I can hope for now is the essay question, friend and only hope of the unprepared. Or matching. I love matching. I'd like to meet the person who invented matching. Levels the playing field. Gives all of us a fighting chance.

Someone moves the chair next to mine and drops into it. That smell. That *presence.* It can't be. But it must be.

"So, are you ready for this?"

I look up, and I'm staring into the most beautiful brown eyes—yes, I'll say it, twinkling eyes—of Jackson House. I don't care what ***Plain Jane*** says. No one on the face of this earth has brown eyes like these.

I am without speech, so I combine two gestures. I shrug and shake my head. At the same time.

This makes him smile, showing perfect white teeth. And a dimple on his left cheek. "Well," he says, "at least we'll go down with smiles on our faces. That was fun last night, Mary Jane."

I want him to say my name again. If I could speak, I would ask him to.

Inside, I'm not only speaking—I'm arguing:

M.J.: *This is so cool! He likes you! He likes you!*

Plain Jane: *The boy is only staring at you because you have a zit forming on the tip of your chin, right where you always get one.*

M.J.: *If he were any hotter, this whole building would burst into flames!*

Plain Jane: *Do you want to lose every last friend you have? Think about Cassie and Samantha and Jessica. Are you going to give up all your real friends for a guy? Lay down your book and step away from the boy!*

M.J.: *Forget everything else. Grab the man and kiss those lips—*

"No talking," orders our teacher, as if speech were an option. He passes out his quiz, starting with the front row.

"Good luck," Jackson whispers right before Schram gets to our row.

Our row. I love the sound of it. *Our row.* Like *our* song. Or *our* house. Or *our* children.

"Miss Ettermeyer?"

I look up at Schram because that's me. Mary Jane Ettermeyer.

"A pencil? Or pen? You'll need one to answer the question." Our teacher says this as if he's repeating it, as if he's been standing there, asking me if I need a pen. I think he *has* been standing there, asking this frivolous question.

I reach for my pack and start to search for pen or pencil,

when one appears in front of my nose. It is held by Jackson House. Oh, lucky, lucky pencil.

"Here. You can use this," he says.

I think I manage to give thanks. Out loud. I take the pencil and can feel the heat of his strong fingers. I clutch Jackson's pencil, lift it to my nose, and inhale. It smells like him, like a forest after the rain. Jackson House has given me his pencil.

I think I'm going to cry again.

When I come to, I glance around the room. At least a dozen pair of eyes are aimed at me. At *us. Us. Us. Us.*

How much did they see? How much do they know?

"You have thirty minutes to answer the essay question with as much information as you can supply," Mr. Schram announces. "You'd better get started."

It's an essay question. *Yes!* Maybe things are turning my way after all.

I straighten myself in my chair, feeling better about my chances of survival than I've felt in forty-eight hours. I can do essay questions. I can sound smart and logical, frequently without knowing anything about what I'm writing about. The trick is to number your points: "There are three main points the reader has to consider when discussing . . ." Knowing names and dates, of course, is always a bonus. But even those can be omitted, with the artful use of *however* and *therefore.* Mix in a little smart-word exchange, like *utilize* for *use,* or *explicit* for *clear, cognitive processing* for *thinking,* that kind of thing. And you're there. At least a C.

Then I read the question.

It's a joke. I look up suddenly, suspiciously. Others are writing. Nicole is chewing on her pencil. Lauren is scribbling a hundred miles an hour. But they must have had a hand in this. It can't be a coincidence.

The essay question is:

Examine the theme of betrayal in "Julius Caesar."

I'm still writing when everybody else appears to be done. It's not that I've written so much. It just took me forever to get over the question.

Mr. Schram comes and stands beside my desk.

"Wow," Nicole says. She acts like she's saying it to Lauren, but she's so loud I hear her clear across the room. "Looks like Mary Jane knows a lot about betrayal."

I stop writing and hand over my paper and wish I were somebody else. Cassie doesn't stand up for me. Neither does Samantha. Or Jessica. ***Plain Jane*** is pretty much agreeing with Nicole (which makes calculating the odds of "them" against "us" next to impossible).

I vow I'll forever stay away from Jackson House. My girlfriends are too important to me. Girlfriends are forever. Nicole is right. How could I have even thought about being with somebody else's boyfriend? I'm not like that. I'm loyal. I'm trustworthy. I'm—

"You can keep the pencil." *He,* Jackson, stands up and smiles at me as if he hasn't heard Nicole. "See ya."

I watch him walk out of the room. I have his pencil. His

gift to me. A token. His words, his *promise*—"See ya"—echoes in my heart. What does he mean by that? "See" as in "seeing each other"?

I will have to ponder those two words. I shall mull them over and over and over, reading between the lines. I will dissect those words within an inch of their lives.

The room has nearly emptied now. Except for Nicole. Cassie and Lauren are hanging by the door, like they're waiting for the show to start.

I don't want a show. I don't want to talk to Nicole. (I am definitely not liking her now. Did I ever like her? Yes, we were on the same tree, but different branches.) I want to go somewhere quiet and ponder *"See ya."*

I move to the door, but Nicole blocks my path. I don't think she's the kind for physical violence, at least not on behalf of someone other than herself. Not that I haven't seen my share of fights at Attila Ill, and the majority of them female. And she does have about an inch and ten pounds on me. And fingernails. But Nicole is too much of a girlie girl for hand-to-hand combat. I think.

M.J.'s voice is the only one talking in my head because ***Plain Jane*** is too scared.

"Nicole," I say, following ***M.J.***'s lead and refusing to cower before the Ambassador, "who are you going out with these days?"

This appears to throw her off guard. She's only here as an ambassador to the Star. Her personal life has nothing to do with the current situation. "I—I don't know," she stammers.

I give her a wan smile, the kind you'd give your mom if she'd ruined her favorite dress and you felt sorry for her, even though it wasn't that much of a dress to start with. "Nobody?" I query. "What about Travis? Aren't you guys still talking?" We all knew about her king-sized crush on Travis the first of the year. I also happen to know that he's been going out with a junior cheerleader since October.

"Travis? No." She tries to collect herself and get back the haughty ambassador look. "What's it to you anyway?"

"I care about you, Nicole. That's all. So shoot me."

"Nicole!" Lauren calls from the doorway. "We're going to be late to chem. I'm leaving."

Nicole is still blocking my path. "You need to talk to Star, Mary Jane. You know she and Jackson are going together."

I smile at Nicole. I could nod and be done with this. That's what I *should* do, what ***Plain Jane*** in my head would very likely tell me to do if she were talking to me. But taking the easy way out is not ***M.J.***'s style. And before I can stop her voice, I'm echoing it: "I know Star and Jackson have been going out, Nicole. *You* know they've been going out. Jackson must know it too, right? Star certainly knows this, at least most of the time, when her *interests* don't lie elsewhere and she's not going out with someone else."

Nicole starts to interrupt, but I won't let her.

"So if it's true love and all," I continue with impeccable logic, "what are you girls so worried about?"

I move around her and take two steps before she wheels on me and shouts, "Just don't forget the way things are around here!" This is tree talk. To Nicole, Star hangs at the top of The Girls' family tree. She is our leader, our guide, the most powerful Girl. If Star decides to claim one guy as hers, with half a dozen guys on the side, then those of us on the lower branches should just go along with it.

I take a deep breath, then turn back to face her. "And you, Nicole, don't forget that the way things are doesn't mean it's the way things are meant to be."

4

Plain Jane vs. Lunch

I walk out of English class, trying to replay what exactly I said to Nicole. I'm grateful that there were no witnesses. Lauren and Cassie must have given up and gone to their classes. I can deny every word, if it comes to that.

But what *did* I say anyway? That the way things are doesn't mean that's the way they're *meant* to be? Was that it? What does that even mean? How are things "meant to be"?

I know how I'd like things to be.

I stick Jackson's pencil into the pocket of my gray sweater and hold on to it.

See ya. See ya. See ya . . .

I must be losing my mind.

Luckily, none of The Girls have second-hour French with

me. Seniors don't usually take beginning French. But I left the class to the last possible minute. My penalty is that I share the room with mostly freshmen and sophomores, who still think French is the language of romance.

Why did I wait so long? Because I don't find French men or their language sexy. Not that I've ever met a French man. Our teacher's name is Mr. Smith. Enough said. Plus, it makes no sense to me why I should be required to have a language (other than my own) to enter college. I don't know what I want to do when I grow up, but I do know that I don't want to do it in France.

Nothing much happens until lunch, which happens at 10:50. This absurd lunch hour is the result of a new security policy adopted by Attila Ill in the wake of all those high school shootings upstate. I'm not sure how eating lunch when normal people are still thinking about breakfast is supposed to make us safer, but Principal Garrison assures us that this is so. We now have shorter lunch periods and more of them. Four, to be exact, with the last group storming around the halls, writhing in hunger pangs, until they are allowed to dine at something like 1:32 p.m.

I put my books in my locker and search the hall for Cassie, but she's not there. This could mean nothing, since about half the time she goes straight from study hall to lunch without passing Go or stopping at her locker.

But I suspect her absence is by design. In high school, one of the major rules is Guilt by Association. You can't be friends with a girl other girls are mad at, or they will automatically transfer said madness to you. Guilt by Association.

If Alicia were still in high school, she would be standing right here at my locker, waiting for me. She'd keep associating, no matter what. Cassie, who isn't half the man Alicia is, is nowhere in sight.

And can you blame the girl? ***Plain Jane*** asks. She is angry. She's been silent most of the morning, worrying about the likely prospect of going through her whole senior year without a single girlfriend.

M.J. isn't saying much either. She's not mad or anything. She's just spending every possible minute thinking about Jackson House and mulling over his last words: "See ya." She is on the lookout for the boy.

I try to pull myself together, to buck up. My mother, Mrs. Thomas S. Ettermeyer, is Queen of the Bucker-Uppers. She demands nothing less of her offspring. On my first day of school, when I refused to get out of the minivan, she issued bucking-up commands intended to carry me through any conceivable difficulty: *Keep your chin up! Don't let them get you down! And above all, remember who you are, Missy. After all is said and done, you are an Ettermeyer, of the Evanston Ettermeyers.*

I try to remember my mother's sage advice as I do the dead-man-walking shuffle to the cafeteria.

Ever since kindergarten, ***Plain Jane*** has been the one who shows up for lunch. The second I step into the lunchroom, she's there, whispering: *You look so stupid. Why did you wear gray? And these jeans? Hello? The seventies called. They want their clothes back. Besides, you know these jeans make you look fat. See that girl over there? The one with guys hanging all over* *her? You will never have hair like that. You will never pull off that air of confidence. Look around you. Admit it. Nobody here wants you to sit with them. Don't even try to put your tray on their table.*

As I stroll between tables to get my food, comically called "hot" lunch, I'm reminded that school cafeterias always make me think of prison. And I'm not just referring to the fact that school kitchens and prison kitchens share the same food supplier in Uncle Sam.

It's not a prison cafeteria our cafeteria reminds me of. It's more like death row. That last march, with all eyes on you. The sneers. The clanging of metal. The catcalls on occasion. The desire to be anywhere else, anyone else.

Alicia saved lunch hour for me. For three wonderful years, I knew I'd always have somebody to sit with at lunch. No matter what happened, we always ate lunch together. We'd drop and add classes if, for some reason, they gave us different lunch periods.

Now I have to face the great unknown every single day. If Cassie comes to her locker after study hall, I have it made. We can walk to lunch together and dump our stuff off at *her* table, the cheerleaders' table. They don't seem to resent me if I appear with her Cassie-ness.

If, on the other hand, as today, I walk in alone, there's a chance I will actually eat alone. Or worse, I could sit at one of the loser tables and still eat alone.

Is there anything more pathetic than being forced to eat alone in a school cafeteria?

I take the pizza, at 10:53 a.m., and walk back to the madding crowd. Star Simons is hovering over the cheerleading table, talking to Cassie, even though Star's supposed to be in the hunger-pang, late-lunch group. *Ha ha.* She's wearing skin-tight jeans and a lime green top that's even tighter and barely covers her bra. Her auburn hair (not her real color) is long and straight, parted on the side. And she's thin. Model thin, coming and going.

Star graciously smiles at The Girls, then dashes out of the cafeteria. Heads turn. Gazes linger.

Plain Jane doesn't miss this opportunity to point out that Star is beautiful. Gorgeous even.

Lauren is seated illegally at the cheerleading table, and so are two juniors who don't cheer and therefore do not deserve or qualify for these expensive seats. So I'm seriously considering sitting in the empty space next to Cassie and pretending nothing is wrong.

I start toward the table, but inside my head, ***Plain Jane*** is screaming, *Stop! Are you crazy? You are so not cheerleader material! Never mind the fact that they're all probably talking about you. You don't belong with those girls.*

She's right. So I turn and scan the room for an empty table. I look left. I look right.

Nothing.

Nowhere to go. Nowhere to hide. I can't eat this pizza on my plate. It's all red, gooey sauce, with almost no cheese on it. And it's 10:56 a.m., for crying out loud.

I smile and nod as I weave between tables. These gestures aren't aimed at anyone in particular, though I'm hoping that if anyone is watching me, it will appear as if I'm greeting all of my many inmate friends scattered around the cafeteria.

I want Alicia.

Why hasn't someone done an exposé on school cafeterias? I'd like to see those investigative reporters uncover corruption and extortion in seating arrangements, not to mention the Mafia behavior of cheerleaders. And the smells? There's no way cafeteria smell comes from anything remotely connected with food. I suspect it's a semipoisonous spray of some sort. Instead of little after-school specials, let's have a reality show on the school lunch hour. It would make that *Survivor* show or *Fear Factor* look like *Mary Poppins.*

Everybody worries about high school dropout rates. I'll tell you why kids drop out of school. Lunch! Take away lunch hour, and watch school attendance soar. Why do we even need lunch hour? It's not an hour. It's barely lunch. Why can't we just eat while we're watching class, like we do at home, only we watch TV?

I keep walking through the cafeteria, because what else am I going to do? Only there are no empty tables. And I've passed the table of no return. The last loser table.

You cannot, under any circumstances, backtrack in a school cafeteria. You might as well hang a sign around your neck that says: FRIENDLESS. WILL WORK FOR FRIEND.

I'm almost back to the last three tables. The infamous tables.

The jock tables.

5

M.J. vs. the Jocks

Brad Hartwell is talking to Tim Collins. But when he sees me, he stops talking and gives me a long, slow smile. I am not imagining this, as I stand before the jock table, tray held in front of me like an offering.

He has to be smiling at somebody behind you, you idiot, **Plain Jane** is quick to point out.

Still, it's making me nervous. Even if he's not smiling at me, this whole table spells trouble. I consider walking away from the jocks and throwing myself on the mercy of my girlfriends, or possibly the losers' table.

But ***M.J.*** reasons, effectively, that a table full of jocks is not necessarily a bad thing. Not at all. Jock interest increases a girl's value, even with The Girls. *Sit with the boys,* ***M.J.*** coaxes. *What could it hurt? They won't bite.*

I manage to smile back at Brad. After all, I've known him through eleven-plus years of classrooms and lunchrooms. Never mind that he's never so much as said "Boo" to me.

Tim is smiling at me, too. ***Plain Jane*** would call it *leering,* but I'm no longer listening to her.

"Take a load off, Mary Jane," Brad says. He scoots over, clearing a spot between Tim and him.

I don't move.

Tim pats the empty spot. "Come on. We promise not to bite."

Hmm. Score one for ***M.J.***

"Yeah," Brad agrees. "C'mon! Lunch is going to be over before you get a chance to enjoy the famous school pizza."

The whole table has stopped talking. I wouldn't be surprised to discover that we are in an alternate reality and the entire cafeteria has been zapped into silence.

Or maybe it's just that the cafeteria noise seems like silence compared to the screaming going on inside my head:

Plain Jane: *Have you looked at yourself in the mirror lately? Your zit is coming into its own. You can't let them see you eat. You're fat, fat, fat! Step away from the table! I'm telling you—this is all a trick, a cruel joke!*

But I'm thinking ***Plain Jane*** is wrong—at least about the joke part. The looks I'm picking up here aren't aimed at my zit. I feel like crossing my arms over my breasts. But since I can't, I raise my lunch tray strategically.

M.J.: *Sweet! These guys like what they see! Sit with them. You can do this! They probably heard how cool you were at Cassie's, and they want to get to know you.*

Plain Jane interrupts at this point: *That's it! Now you've done it. These boys have heard about you, the way you threw yourself at Star's boyfriend last night, staying out until all hours. I knew this was going to happen. They all want to sit by you because you're easy!*

M.J.: *You're easy! You're easy! They think you're easy! They all want to sit by you! You've finally made it! You're popular!*

M.J. is crazy. I am so not popular. Or easy.

Finally, because my knees are starting to weave, I sit down, taking the open spot between Tim and Brad. It's a smaller space than I'd banked on, and I'm touching both jocks, not that I'm complaining. But I feel a bit like a twig in a Christmas tree lot.

"So, Mary Jane," Brad says, leaning over and smelling my tray of prison food. As he does this, he brushes against my arm. "What's for lunch?"

"Pizza," I answer cleverly.

M.J. is shouting: *You will never in your whole life get a chance like this! Take advantage of it, or I'm never speaking to you again. Go for it!*

Plain Jane has always insisted that the way to a man's heart is through his stomach, so I say, "There's no way I'm eating pizza for breakfast. Anybody want mine?"

Seven hands appear on my tray. The winning hand belongs

to a sophomore, one of the few sophomores on the varsity team, John Something. He snatches the pizza and takes a bite, devouring half the slice in one jerky motion. Red oozes down his chin.

"So what brings you to our neck of the woods?" Tim asks.

"I believe it was Brad," I answer, feeling the power of ***M.J.*** behind my words. "Couldn't resist his charm, when he so sweetly said, 'Take a load off.' "

They laugh. I'm being funny with a tableful of jocks.

They're laughing at *you!* **Plain Jane** cries.

They're laughing with *you!* ***M.J.*** insists.

"That's right, Tim," Brad agrees. "You can take notes from the master. Maybe one day you, too, can get a hottie to sit by you."

Tim reaches behind me and punches Brad in the shoulder. "Hey! Last time I looked, I *did* have a hottie sitting next to me."

They are talking about *me! I* am the hottie Tim just punched Brad over.

M.J. is purring.

"What are they staring at?" John asks, motioning to a B-level senior girls' table.

I look and see six pairs of eyes focused on me. I choose to ignore them for now.

"They're probably wondering who the new jock is," Brad jokes. He elbows my rib. It hurts a little.

"You think I couldn't make your ol' football team if I wanted to?" I ask, as if offended.

"You?" Tim laughs. "You wouldn't last two seconds on the

field." He flicks his fingers, like he's flicking a fly. "You'd be facedown in the dirt with footprints on your jersey."

"First of all," I say, setting the stale cookies from my tray to the middle of the table and letting the guys fight over them, "we'd all get new outfits. Seriously, does anyone look good in black and gold? And the shoulder pads have got to go. Out with the eighties. Second of all, doesn't everybody end up facedown in the dirt sooner or later in that game? So when you stop doing that, and when you get some decently spun threads, then you can give me a call for tryouts."

I have them all laughing. ***Plain Jane*** is yelling at me. She wants me to look around the cafeteria. She's sure every girlfriend is watching and disapproving. But ***M.J.*** is trying to convince her that flirting with the entire team is a good thing. Then Star won't take flirting with Jackson so personally.

"Seriously," Tim says, "how come you walked up to our table?"

"Okay, Tim. I'll tell you. But you have to keep it a secret."

They're quiet, all two tons of jocks leaning in to hear.

"I'm conducting a psych experiment. It's for my psychology class. I'm trying to prove that jocks can, too, do two things at once, like eat and talk."

Half of them groan. Half of them laugh.

Brad's in my psych class, but I wonder if he knows it because we've never talked before today.

"We're not doing psych experiments in that class," Brad says, answering my unspoken question about whether or not he knows we're in the same class. He knows.

"Extra credit," I insist. "You'd know this if you didn't sleep so much in class."

This gets approving *oohs* and *ouches* from my jock fans.

Brad turns to Tim. "She calls our prof 'Sigh Fry.'" Then he turns back to me. "Tell 'em why."

I'm stunned that Brad knows my pet name for our teacher, Geraldine Fry. But I recover from this information and turn to the mass of jocks hanging on my every word. "Okay. Her last name's Fry, so that part should be easy, even for you, Tim." I get the laughter I so richly deserve. I am on a roll here. "The first part is tougher, so pay attention. This woman starts every answer to every question with a deep, soul-shaking sigh. For example, Brad here might ask, 'What do you call it when you think somebody's out to get you?' And Sigh Fry will give this deep sigh, as if to say, 'What did I do to deserve this classroom of idiots?' and then answer, 'Paranoid.' Hence, she is dubbed 'Sigh,' as in 's-i-g-h' Fry."

"Excellent," Tim says, nodding.

I don't eat one bite of food the entire lunch hour, but I've never had a better lunch in my entire life.

Kids at other tables are getting up and dumping trash when Brad whispers to me, "I hear you had a real good time with Jackson last night."

My throat goes dry. Something about the way he said it makes me want to hear ***Plain Jane*** in my head. But she isn't speaking to me. So I have to go with ***M.J.*** But my stomach feels like I've just eaten pizza sauce for breakfast, even though I haven't.

"I try to have a good time wherever I am and whoever I'm with." I wave my hand over the jock table. "Case in point."

"Oooh," Tim croons as he climbs off the bench and lifts his tray. "Mary Jane's a good time for all."

As I dump the lunch remains into the trash can, I can't believe I just said what I did. I didn't mean it—not *that* way. Not Tim's way. I think I'm going to hurl as I imagine those words scrawled on bathroom walls throughout Attila Ill:

CALL MARY JANE—A GOOD TIME FOR ALL.

6

Intrigue

Dazed, I spend the entire next hour contemplating my reputation, instead of contemplating the sociology of third-world countries like everybody else in my political science class. Could my reputation possibly be up for grabs—over four minutes? *Four* missing minutes?

I've never had to think much about my reputation. I used to feel like I was the only student at Attila Ill who hadn't done *it*. According to guys, they've all had sex 137 times by the time they enter high school. Girls may not brag about *it* as much as guys (I mean, that would be impossible), but rumors fly, and girls don't deny. Nobody wants to be seen as a player, but you don't want to be the only puritan left either.

It was my friend Alicia who set me straight. She said that, contrary to the juice coming from the school grapevine, most high school girls haven't done *it*. They just don't admit the fact. The night before Alicia started high school, she and I and a friend of hers named Red, short for Rianna Elizabeth Douglas, made a pact to "save ourselves" for the one true love of our lives. Well, one for each of us.

Since then, I've managed to secure dates for most of the major high school events, and I've had guys take me out for movies and hamburgers and parties. But I've never really had the opportunity to break the pact. So my so-called reputation has been a nonissue.

Until now.

I finger Jackson's pencil approximately 736 times the rest of the afternoon and avoid direct eye contact with males and females alike. I don't have to pay for my lunch sins until the end of the day, when I have last-hour study hall with Jessica and Cassie.

Nobody should be forced to spend the last hour of school in the library. They can't possibly think anyone will study. It's not the last minute for any class. What's the use?

The Girls and I sit in the back corner behind the biggest books, the reference shelves. That way we are farthest away from Ms. Lake, who looks so much like a librarian should that I suspect she's impersonating one and one day we'll find out she's a wanted serial ax murderer hiding out from the FBI. Her round face is the epitome of pleasant, framed by curly, dark hair. She wears silk scarves every day with library memorabilia on them, like books and library cards.

When Ms. Lake interrupts our library conversations, she does so with index finger pressed to her thin lips as she whispers, "Quiet, please!"

You have to love this woman, ax murderer or no, symbol of the American library.

I make a pit stop in the girls' bathroom before reporting to the library. You couldn't pay me to actually use the johns in this room, of course. I'd rather my sides split from holding it. I just need a minute to collect myself before facing The Girls in study hall.

Nobody's in the john, except a group of freshmen girls, who don't know any better. As I wash my hands at the sink, I watch them in the mirror and wonder if I was ever that young and carefree.

I glimpse myself in the smudged glass reflection, and for one second I don't recognize this stranger drying her hands on a paper towel. I can't look away from her as she stares back at me. Inside my head, voices are describing what I'm looking at, Mary Jane Ettermeyer:

***Plain Jane**: Average. Average height. Nothing remarkable about her face, except for the zit on her chin. Brown eyes (like three-quarters of the known Homo sapiens). Good eyesight. Brown hair. Lips are too big. Doesn't look good in anything she wears. Nothing to write home about.*

***M.J.:** 34C. Nice rear end. Sexy. Hot even. Desirable. Jeans could be tighter. Should have used Flame Red lipstick on those luscious lips.*

If I'm ever wanted by the police, I hope the voices in my head are the only witnesses to the crime. I'd like them to be the ones describing me to the police artist. Nobody would ever catch Mary Jane Ettermeyer.

I tell Ms. Lake I'm sorry as I arrive late to study hall. She shakes her head and gives me a sweet smile, undoubtedly so that I won't suspect her real profession, ax murdering. Still, I'm less afraid of her than I am of The Girls, who are waiting for me, just as I knew they would be.

"Hey, guys," I call, taking the seat between Cassie and Jessica, the chair they've obviously left for me. It feels a bit like taking the witness stand.

Samantha is on the other side of Jessica. She's no more firmly entrenched in the popular group than I am and has been known to flit from branch to branch. But she's in on this, whatever *this* is.

I glance down at Cassie's feet. "Sweet! Great kicks, Cassie."

This momentarily puts her off track. "You think?" She raises her crossed leg so she can admire her new shoes. They're Doc Martens. "I loved them in the store," she explains. "Now I'm not so sure. You think they go with jeans?"

She's wearing Levi's, and the shoes don't go.

"Yeah," I lie. "They're so fly. Wish I had a pair like them." Which I would only wear if I were dead.

Jessica clears her throat with meaning.

"Anyway," Cassie begins, "we need to talk, Mary Jane. I don't think you have any idea what people are saying about you."

"Me?" The surprise in my voice isn't fake. I'm an under-the-radar kind of gal. The thought of people talking about me makes me have to swallow three times before I can breathe normally.

"Seriously, Mary Jane," Jessica chimes in. "What's gotten into you?"

I look from Jessica, to Samantha, to Cassie. There's concern there, worry even. And friendship. I feel like I'm slipping, falling.

Samantha leans in front of Jessica and whispers, "What were you thinking? Why would you sit at the jock table?"

"I know." I stare down at my hands, hands that fed jocks. The Girls are getting to me. They're melting my defenses. I can feel it happening. I have to bite my lip to keep back the tears. I love these people. I need them to like me.

"You're right." I look to Cassie. "I don't know how it happened. I—I knew you guys didn't want me at *your* table. I was so upset. I didn't know where to go."

"What do you mean we didn't want you at our table?" Cassie demands.

"Because everybody hates me now!" My voice cracks as I say it. And it's so loud that the ax murderer glances our way.

Cassie puts her hand on my arm. "We don't hate you!" she insists.

"How could you think that?" Jessica seconds.

"We're just worried about you," Samantha adds.

"You're not mad?" I ask, amazed, relieved, repentant.

"How could we be mad at you?" Cassie asks, squeezing my arm. "But . . ."

I knew there would be a *but,* and I brace myself.

"But," Cassie continues, "you've got to get a grip, girl. It's like you're edging toward a cliff or something. You're in self-destruct mode."

"And Nicole's right," Samantha says. "Star really is hurt."

"Why?" I ask, wondering how Samantha knows this. "Because of Jackson? Jackson wasn't even at the jock table."

"Not about lunch," Samantha explains, which proves she's been talking to Star. "About last night. Things are really messed up."

M.J. has about thirty-seven defensive comebacks for the branch hopper. She's shouting all of them to my brain at once. I will not listen to ***M.J.***, though. She's the one who got me into this mess in the first place.

"Make it right, Mary Jane," Cassie advises in a therapeutic tone of voice.

"What am I supposed to do?" The question is rhetorical. I think.

"*Talk* to Star."

This suggestion sounds about as inviting as "Pet the snake."

"It's the only way," Jessica chimes in.

"Tell her you're sorry," Cassie continues.

If you ask me, Star should be the one telling Jackson *she's* sorry for dating behind his back. But nobody asks me, so I keep my thoughts to myself.

Cassie is relentless. "Tell her she's got nothing to worry about."

I sigh, realizing that this is undoubtedly true and wondering if it would kill me to admit it to Star.

Cassie squeezes my arm again. "Mary Jane, I really think you need to do this. It's our senior year. I just want us all to get along and have the best year ever. We've waited our whole lives for this. Don't screw it up."

Cassie says this so earnestly that I find myself agreeing with her. I'm nodding. I want a great senior year, too.

"Don't look now, but Lauren's watching you," Jessica whispers.

I look. Can't help myself. Lauren's pretending to read her history book, but I can see her seeing me.

"Do it, Mary Jane," Cassie whispers. "Talk to Star fast, before this goes any further."

By the time study hall is over, I've made my decision. No doubt I will continue to long for Jackson House, to cherish his pencil, perhaps even to write his name in my diary, if I start keeping a diary. But I will hide these things inside for the sake of The Girls, of whom I am one. Not only that, but I'll make peace. The ***Plain Jane*** in me can hardly believe that Star actually feels threatened by me. But I don't want to take any chances. I'll talk to Star for the good of the family tree, to root out the discord and let us all blossom into our senior year.

Star's locker is in the east hall, so I get my things out of my locker and hurry down the hall, hoping I'm not too late. I want to get this over with.

She's at her locker, squatting in front of it, reaching for something. Star Simons really is the prettiest girl at Attila Ill. Her auburn hair looks as great now as it did in the morning, bouncy and shiny, shampoo-commercial hair.

I walk up to her. "Hey, Star."

She looks up. If she's surprised to see me, it doesn't show.

She gets up, carrying a stack of books. The smile on her face looks real enough and gives me the courage I need to go on and do what I've got to do. It may be my imagination, but I can feel all eyes upon us.

I clear my throat. "Star, there's a lot of crazy talk going on around here today."

She cocks her head slightly to one side. Her eyes narrow ever so slightly. Her smile is immovable.

"Well, I don't know what you've heard," I say, stumbling on with it. "You know. About me. About Jackson. About me and Jackson. Or whatever."

That head tilts a bit more. Smile still in place.

I forge ahead. "Anyways. I just wanted to tell you myself that I'm sorry, like if you heard something stupid that made you think anything was going on. Like with Jackson and me or anything. Because I'd never do anything to hurt you."

The smile gets bigger, but somehow I'm not relieved.

"So really that's all," I say. "We're okay then. Right?"

She smiles deeply and shifts the books she's holding. Then, without changing her expression, with that smile still beaming, she whispers, "Wrong. We are *not* okay."

Chills invade my body as my blood turns to ice.

Star flashes me another smile and turns to go. "See you, Mary Jane!" she calls back to me, so friendly, so nice, that for a minute I wonder if I dreamed the last ten seconds, like a streak of lightning that flashes in a clear sky, leaving you to doubt your own eyes once it's gone.

Did Star really say what I thought she said? *We are* not *okay.*

7

Bullies

I'm still replaying my scene with Star as I wait in line to drive out of the senior parking lot. The voices in my head agree that I really did see what I thought I saw, the evil Star poking through the pseudosweet one. They just can't agree what I should do about the vision.

You should have decked Star Simons right there in the hall! ***M.J.*** insists.

But did you see how beautiful Star was, even when she gave you that evil look? ***Plain Jane*** points out. *Maybe you should get your hair cut like hers.*

I want Alicia.

I fumble for my cell, find it, and hit my #1 speed dial.

As it rings, I picture Alicia sitting in class, her phone ringing in her big flowered bag. She's always rejected backpacks and conventional book bags. Surely college couldn't have changed her that much. She's only been gone a few months, but it feels like years.

"What?" It's Alicia's voice, but she sounds sleepy. And angry. Maybe out of breath.

"Alicia? It's me. Mary Jane."

"Just a minute."

Muffled voices. One of them male.

I picture Alicia, petite, five feet two, blonde hair pulled up into a ponytail. Bright blue eyes and teeny nose. She was the kind of girl guys would see and want to hug and protect. But talk to her for two seconds, and you'd know she didn't need a guy to protect her. She dated a lot in high school. But she never had a real boyfriend. And she was fine with it.

She comes back to the phone. "Sorry, Mary Jane. Can you hang on a minute?"

"Is this a bad time, Alicia?" I ask.

Somebody, a guy, laughs in the background. "No!" he shouts, and I hear him over the phone. "It's a great time! Just not to talk."

"Shut up!" Alicia says, but not to me, and she's laughing.

Plain Jane is whining in my head. *You shouldn't be bothering Alicia. Obviously, she's moved on. She always was cooler than you.*

I wish I hadn't called. "Alicia?" I shout. "I'll call back. Are you—?"

"There." The only voice I hear on the other end of the line now is hers. "Sorry about that."

"Who *was* that?" I ask.

"Colt. Can you believe it? That's his real name, Mary Jane. Colton Caldwell. Doesn't that sound like somebody we'd make up for a short story?"

"Yeah," I agree. I'm not sure what else to say, how to start. Alicia and I have always been able to talk about anything. She's understood me better than anybody I've ever known, including the rents. But now I don't know what to say?

"Listen, Mary Jane. I've been meaning to call you. Well, first, I was going to wait until Thanksgiving to tell you, so we could hug and make girl sounds. But I can't wait."

"Wait for what?"

"I am in love!"

There's silence. I know I should be making girl sounds, but they won't come.

"I know," she continues. "Shocker, huh? Alicia, the nonbeliever-in-love. I just hadn't met Colt, I guess. Not that there are any guys like him in high school."

"Wow," I manage.

"You said it," she says. "This is the real thing. I've never felt anything like this. He's . . . he's perfect, Mary Jane."

"Perfect is good."

"I want you to meet him. Hey! Maybe I can bring him

home with me over Thanksgiving break! I've told him all about you." Pause. "On the other hand, I'm not sure he's ready to meet the rents." Pause. "On the other hand, I don't think I could go four days without seeing him!" Pause.

"That would be good," I say. "I mean, if I met him. I want to meet him." I pull onto Center Street and head for Roy Dale Special School for my sister's game. "I should really call you back. I'm not great talking and driving."

"Where are you anyway?" she asks.

"In Fred. Headed to Sandy's basketball game."

"Man, I miss her games! I miss Sandy. I even miss Fred. Tell your sister good luck for me, okay? Go, Dragons! And if she's got a game over Thanksgiving, I'm there! Ooh—Colt, too! He would love a Special Olympics basketball game!"

"Okay."

She starts to punch off. Then she hollers, "Wait! You still there?"

"I'm here."

"So why did you call me? What's up? You go for three weeks without talking to me—"

"We've e-mailed," I interrupt, not sure why I feel accused when she's the one who barely e-mails and never calls.

"Tell! What's wrong? Man, I'm sorry, Mary Jane. How *me-me-me* of me. Talk."

This sounds like the old Alicia, and it makes me want to crawl inside my cell to be with her.

"Do you remember Jackson House?" I ask.

"Yeah."

Silence.

"*You* and Jackson House?" she exclaims. "He's so hot! Way to go, Mary Jane!"

"It's not like that. He's still going with Star. Kind of. I guess. I just—"

"Well," she interrupts, "does *he* feel the same way you do?"

"I don't know." I almost cruise past Sandy's school and have to turn fast, without signaling, to make the drive. Someone behind me honks. "I'm at Roy Dale, Alicia. I've got to go. I'll call you tonight, okay?"

"You sure you're okay till then?"

I grin into the phone. "I'm sure."

"Okay. But call me. I want to hear everything."

I flip the phone off and jog into Roy Dale.

Roy Dale Special School has the feel of an old elementary school. It's a small brick one-story building, where even though the sign says you have to check in at the office before you can go anywhere, it's okay if you don't. I wave to Madeline, who's been the office person ever since Sandy started going to Roy Dale.

It was a good move, changing her from the regular school to this one. Here, she's a star. When she went to my old elementary school, she was low man on the totem pole of lows.

That's actually how Alicia and I first got to be friends. It was all because of Sandy. Alicia was in fourth grade, I was in third, and Sandy was mainstreamed to fifth grade, although she spent most of her time in the special class.

It was close to the beginning of the year, I think. I was waiting for Sandy at the school's main door so I could walk her home. When she was late, I backtracked to her last class, an adapted history class that was still way over her head. It was her semi-mainstream class and the only class she didn't like.

She wasn't in the history room, so I figured she had to be back in her special classroom. I stormed back for her, hacked off that she was making me late. But she wasn't there.

I remember the panic starting to take over. I ran down the hall, calling, "Sandy! Sandy!"

Then I heard somebody shouting. Only it wasn't Sandy's voice. Somebody was screaming, "Leave her alone! Stop it! I mean it. You leave her alone!"

I ran toward the voice, knowing Sandy was in the middle of something horrible.

I rounded the corner and can still picture the scene. Three of the bigger boys, who were probably from Sandy's history class, were circling her like hungry wolves. Sandy stood in the middle, her books and coat at her feet, her hands covering her ears.

"Come on, retard!" the biggest boy was saying. "Just one little kiss and we'll let you go home to your mommy."

The other two boys laughed and kept moving in circles around Sandy.

And there, standing up to them, even though she wasn't half their size, was Alicia. "Stop it, you idiots!" she screamed. "Or you'll be sorry!" She ran at the biggest boy, Mark Something, and rammed her head into his stomach.

He grabbed his belly, which was fat, and doubled over.

The other two boys stopped circling.

I guess I was so shocked that I hadn't moved. But I snapped out of it and ran to stand next to this blonde girl, who was a little shorter than I was. "Get out of here!" I shouted at them. I raised my fist. I'd never hit anyone in my whole life, but I would have. "Leave my sister alone!"

Alicia and I stood there, a tiny wall against boys twice our size.

"Back off!" The wiry kid I knew was in fifth grade, Blake, stepped toward us. "Unless you little girls want to give us a kiss, too?"

"You try to kiss any of us," Alicia said, "and I'll break your face."

Blake didn't laugh. I think he believed her. I know I did.

I stepped past them, grabbed Sandy, and pulled her behind us. I could hear her sobbing.

"Get 'em!" Mark hollered, still holding his belly.

"You do," I promised, "and I'll tell the principal, who just happens to be my dad's best friend." That part was a lie, a quick-on-your-feet lie Alicia admired later.

It was a standoff that seemed to last forever. I remember thinking how weird it was that nobody else was around. Like where did principals and teachers go when you needed them for anything bigger than yelling at you for running in the halls?

Then the kid who hadn't said anything did. "Come on, you guys. Let's get out of here."

Blake took a couple of steps backward. "Yeah. Okay. This is stupid."

Mark's face was bright red. "Where are you going?" he screamed after his buddies, who were running down the hall now. When he turned back to us, he didn't look so brave. "Go on! Get her out of here. Who wants to kiss a retard anyway?"

"You're right, you idiot," Alicia said. "Nobody will ever want to kiss *you!*"

That was Alicia. That's why I've missed her so much.

And as I make my way to the Roy Dale gym, I've got a feeling that sooner or later, I'm going to wish I had her standing by me again, facing off the bullies.

8

The Dragons

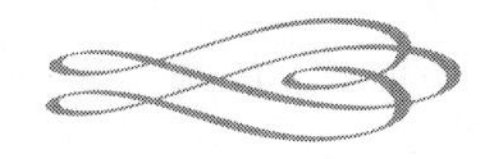

"*Marwyjan!*" *Sandy cries* her own special version of my name and leaves the basketball court when she sees me walk in. They haven't started the real game yet, although my sister would have left the court to greet me even if they had.

I hold out my arms, and she barrels into me for a hug, as if it's been years since we've seen each other, instead of hours. The voices in my head shout, *Hug her back!* and I do. Loving Sandy is one of the few things my voices agree on.

"Purple!" she shouts, stepping back and holding out the sides of her basketball shorts like they're her ballet skirt. Her thin brown hair falls carelessly to her shoulders. She has the face of an angel.

"Very purple," I say. Purple is and always has been Sandy's favorite color. "New uniforms? They look great, Sandy!" I spin her around so I can see the back of her uniform, where it says DRAGONS and 55. "Go, Dragons!" I shout. "Oh, and I talked to Alicia, and she said to tell you good luck and go, Dragons."

Sandy jumps twice and looks toward the door. "Is she coming? Is 'Licia coming?"

"No. She's away at school. Remember? But she's coming home for Thanksgiving, and she wants to see you play."

Michelle, the new coach for the Dragons, keeps glaring over at us. Our last coach, Jeff, was all about the kids. This one's all about winning.

"You better go back with your team," I tell Sandy.

But I barely get the words out when I hear thundering tennis shoes. I look up to see Sandy's buddies stampeding over to us.

"Mary Jane! Mary Jane!" Leslie cries in her soft voice.

Brent, Eric, Chris, and John are way taller than I am. They're all trying to tell me different things at the same time: "Watch me!" "I made a basket last time!" "I shoot!"

We're having our own unofficial team huddle on the sidelines. Jerry, the shortest player, never talks. He just whispers things I can't understand, whispers intently at me, then pats me on the head.

I pretend to fall backward and tumble to the floor, taking Sandy with me. She laughs—loud and without a trace of self-consciousness. Her laugh reminds me of geese honking. It's impossible to hear it and not laugh, too. I'd do almost anything for that laugh . . . and have.

Jerry and Eric fall on top of Sandy and me. The rest of them follow suit until we're in a football pileup on the basketball floor. I laugh so hard I can't stop.

I haven't even felt like laughing since . . . since . . . since the last time I came to one of Sandy's games.

There are no arguments in my head. Nobody's shouting. I could stay like this, wrapped in a cocoon of Sandy-ness, forever.

"Back to the free throw line!" Michelle stands frowning over us. "Come on! Game starts in fifteen." She points to the free-throw line to make sure the kids know exactly which line she wants them to go to. Here, the free-throw line goes by many names. Sandy calls it "the mistake spot."

Sandy gets up and hugs Michelle before shuffle-trotting off. You can tell Michelle isn't the huggy type. The others pile off of me and follow Sandy. Chris, the Dragons' star player, hustles up to walk next to my sister, and not for the first time I wonder if he *likes* her, as in *like* likes her. I uncurl and get to my feet. "Hey, Michelle. Great uniforms."

"We're two short," she says. "We better get them by the Richmond game."

"That the big game this year?" I ask.

"It's the only game I think we could have trouble with," Michelle confides. "We could win district this year. If we can beat Richmond, we could play at ISU."

"Yeah? Well, I'm sure the kids will come through." I can see how desperately she wants this. "So when's the big game?"

"The day after Thanksgiving. Pretty foul timing. I think Carl had something to do with it. He's the coach at Richmond. He's so arrogant. They've won the last three years, and he thinks it will go on forever. Well, not this year."

The visiting team's coach blows a whistle, and the players on that side of the court file back to their benches.

Michelle runs back to our team and herds them to the sidelines.

Alex James is standing by to help get the Dragons settled onto the home team benches. Alex is Red's boyfriend. She's the one who signed the three-way-virgin pact with Alicia and me right before they started high school. Red dubbed us Abstinence in Action, which was pretty funny, since the whole point was *no* action. She and Alex started dating three weeks later.

I watch Alex with Chris, Red's brother and the Dragons' ace scorer. Alex is so good with the kids. "Hey, Alex!" I call.

He pats Chris on the back, then jogs over to me. "Thought you might be here," he says. "Sandy looks good. She been healthy?"

I nod. "How about Chris?"

He grins. "I'd say Chris thinks Sandy looks good, too."

I punch his arm. I do not want to think of Sandy ever going through what I'm going through. "So where's Red?" Red is the Dragons' biggest, or at least most vocal, fan. She almost refused to take a scholarship to a great private school upstate, just because she never wanted to miss any of Chris's games. That, and the fact that she and Alex are mad crazy in love, and he's staying in town and getting an engineering degree from Tri-Community College.

"Red couldn't get home. I had to promise to call her every time Chris scores. She'll be here for the Galion game, though."

"Cool."

"Mary Jane!" Mom's calling me from the top of the six-row bleachers.

I wave up at her. "I better get a seat. Later." Then I start climbing the bleachers. I would never acknowledge my parents at an Attila game, much less sit with them. But the rules of high school don't apply here. This life, these kids, it's all a world inside a world, set apart from everything else. We sit with moms at Roy Dale, and nobody cares.

"Where's Dad?" I ask as I settle next to Mom. She's wearing jeans and a sweatshirt that advertises her real estate company. The main office gave HOUSE HUNTERS shirts away at open houses last year. Oddly enough, we have a dozen of them in every color.

"He's running late, but he said he'll get here as soon as he can."

We watch as the green and purple starting teams gather in the middle of the court. And the game is on.

Nobody scores until the last minute of the first period,

when Chris puts one in from the side. Cheers break out—on both sides. Everybody on the court congratulates Chris, even a couple of guys from the green team. I see Alex holding up his cell to catch the crowd noise, and I know Red's on the other end, screaming just as loud. There is something very right about those two.

Jeff, our last coach, used to make sure everybody on the team got a chance to play and usually in the first period. Not Michelle. She keeps the good players in as long as possible.

Sandy gets to play in the second period, and Dad shows up just as she's walking onto the court. Her eyes are searching the gym for him as she strolls out. When she spots him, she waves and yells, "Hi, Daddy! I get to play!" Then she holds her shorts like she did for me and shouts, "Purple!"

Dad waves and shouts back, "Go, Dragons!" because Sandy has told us we can't say "Go, Sandy," only "Go, Dragons!" Then he bounds up in the stands and sits with Mom and me.

"So we're winning," he says, grinning at our 2–0 rout.

Michelle yells at Sandy to move on the court. For the next ten minutes, Sandy thunders back and forth with her team, but she never touches the ball. Nobody passes it to her. And she's too polite to fight for it.

One of the green players, number 11, a skeleton of a boy, with knees as knobby as baseballs and a shaved head, keeps watching Sandy. Whenever he catches her attention, he breaks into a big smile. Sandy smiles back, and it's almost more than the kid can handle. It's like he can't take his eyes off her.

But Sandy is focused on that ball. She runs up and down the court with everybody else and holds out her arms. The two best Dragon players, Chris and Matt, hog the ball, as usual, passing it back and forth, both of them shooting. Our old coach used to make them pass it to other team members, even though they were the only ones who ever scored.

I feel so bad for Sandy. Her arms are outstretched. Her face is filled with hope that they'll throw her the ball. She gets wide open under the basket, and still the boys act like they only see each other.

Then something happens. The ball skids out of Chris's hands and rolls toward Sandy. She dives for the ball, but the knobby-kneed number 11 green player gets there first. He grabs the ball, dribbles, then stops. His teammates keep running down the court, followed by Dragon defenders, leaving him and Sandy alone on that end.

He grins at Sandy.

She grins back.

Both coaches are screaming.

His teammates are calling for the ball.

Then Green Number 11 kind of hands the ball to Sandy and smiles, as if he's giving her flowers.

Sandy gives him a smile of thanks as she takes the basketball from him. Then she turns and looks up into the bleachers until her gaze settles on me. Her eyes are big, questioning, as if asking permission. I nod. She shrugs. Then she dribbles once, shoots, and scores.

The fans go wild. We're all on our feet, cheering and laughing. Everybody loves it, even the green team parents and fans. And nobody looks happier than the skinny kid with a crush on my sister.

Michelle leaves Sandy in for another five minutes, but Sandy's focus is gone. She tries to follow the ball, moving down the court and up the court as soon as she realizes everybody else is on the move. But she keeps smiling up into the stands at us. And we smile back because you can't help yourself. Everybody's smiling at a Special Olympics game. They should make it a law that every human has to attend one once a month. There would be no more road rage, no NBA basketball brawls.

Sandy goes back to the bench, where she stays until the end of the fourth period. The score has risen to 14 to 2, our lead, but Michelle still hasn't played all the kids. Dad won't let me go down there and have a little talk with her about this. But I think somebody does because all at once she puts in the last four kids, plus Sandy.

Both purple and green teams cheer for the new players. One of the Dragons, Isaac, has only one arm, but he's a good shot. I've seen him sink layups before. Two of the new Dragon players are girls who are still in middle school. They hold hands and look pretty scared. The fourth, Larry, won't come out onto the court. He's autistic. Most of the time we can't get him to leave the bench. He's usually okay in practice. In fact, if he can be on the court all by himself, he's a deadeye shot. I watched him sink eleven three-pointers in a row one day.

Michelle tries to coax him inbounds, but he groans at her and starts rocking back and forth, getting louder, so she leaves him alone.

There's a jump ball. Everybody misses, and the ball rolls right to Sandy's feet.

Dad jumps up and yells, "Honey! Pick it up!"

Sandy smiles up into the stands. Then she bends down and picks up the ball.

"Dribble!" Michelle screams.

Sandy smiles. Then she dribbles once and hugs the ball, still grinning. She says something we can't hear. Then she bounces the ball to Larry, who's still out of bounds.

Larry catches the ball and stops swaying. He smiles at Sandy, who's clapping like crazy. Several of her teammates are clapping, too. So is one from the green team.

The whistle blows. The ball, of course, is out of bounds. Larry allows the referee to take the basketball. Then he starts swaying again.

"You're good, Larry!" Sandy shouts.

"One of these days before too long," Mom says, "we're going to get that boy all the way inbounds. You just wait and see."

We win 14 to 4. But when the game's over both teams hug each other as if they've all won and were all on the same team. And I guess, in a way, we are.

The rents are taking Sandy out for hamburgers, but I pass

on the invitation to join them. I walk out the main doors of Roy Dale and head for my car. I'm not ten feet away when the voices are back at it:

Plain Jane: *What's wrong with you? Couldn't you spare one night to have dinner with your family? Of course you wouldn't want to actually eat a hamburger, since you could stand to lose a couple pounds, you know. But couldn't you at least spend time with them?*

M.J.: *Don't waste another minute thinking about stupid hamburgers! You know exactly what you want to do. Go directly home. Do not pass Go.*

Call Jackson House.

9

Dueling Phones

I lie on my bed, cell in hand, and stare at the black ceiling. Black, because in a fit of angst right before the start of my senior year, I redecorated my room, starting with the ceiling. ***M.J.*** had always wanted a totally black room. Fortunately, ***Plain Jane***'s voice kicked in before I had a chance to extend my black motif to the walls and floor.

I was halfway through blackening my ceiling and had decided it was a huge mistake when Mom walked in.

"Mary Jane!" she cried. "What is wrong with you? Only sick, sick, sick people paint their ceilings black. Are you taking drugs?"

Her reaction pretty much sealed my fate. "I love the black

ceiling, Mom. And you said I could decorate any way I wanted to. It's *my* room. And no. Not taking drugs. But thanks so much for asking."

She left, but she sent Dad.

He stood in the doorway, staring in. "Your mother wants me to tell you that your room is still part of my house," he said evenly. "Our house. Just tell me you're not planning to paint the whole room black."

I managed a nervous laugh. "Of course not, Dad."

He nodded and backed away.

Alicia hadn't left for college yet, so I made her come over. She'd seen in a magazine how some college kids had painted their dorm rooms with sponges, so the walls looked like marble, or cement, depending on the sponge. All I had was black paint, so she hijacked a gallon of white from her stepdad's garage. He was too lazy to paint, so he'd never miss it. Then we mixed black and white and dipped sponges and turned my bedroom walls into gray marble cement. It all turned out okay, but I won't miss my room when I'm off to ISU.

For the tenth time, I punch in Jackson's phone number, which I've looked up and now memorized. But for the tenth time, I click END, instead of SEND. What would I say if he answered?

***M.J.:** Hey, handsome. Let's quit dancing around each other and let Fate have her way with both of us. Meet me in fifteen. See ya.*

Plain Jane: *Tell the truth. You are so not interested in me, right? When you said "See ya," you didn't mean a thing by it, except maybe out of pity. I totally understand.*

I pick up the pencil Jackson gave me. It's white, like his teeth. There's not a toothmark on it. I inhale the smell of lead and wood, close my eyes, and think of his deep brown eyes, his enormous arms and shoulders.

I am so going to call him. I punch in the number again and stare at my cell screen.

The phone rings. The real phone on my bedside table. I'm so shocked that I drop my cell. The phone rings again. I stare at it.

Finally, I pick it up. "Hello?"

"Hey!" It's Alicia's "hey," and I feel my muscles relax.

"Hey, Alicia."

"How'd Sandy do?"

"They won."

"Great! Go, Dragons! Was Red there?"

"Nope. Alex was, though."

"I got an e-mail from Red. She said Alex is working an eight-hour shift and taking eighteen credit hours. And he still has time to IM her constantly."

Red and Alex's relationship has always been a topic of conversation for Alicia and me. "True love, I guess."

"Mmmm," she agrees, as if she deeply understands now. "True love."

I change the subject. "Sandy's psyched about having you at her game. They've got a big one the day after Thanksgiving. I told her you'd be there."

"And so will Colt! We're on. I told him all about Sandy and the games. He can't wait to see one."

"Great." I try to sound like I mean it, but I'm already feeling like I've lost something.

"So," Alicia says, "tell. Don't leave anything out. I want to know every juicy detail about Jackson House."

I give her the unedited version, including all the grief everybody gave me after the night at Cassie's and the scene with Nicole in English class when Jackson came back to sit with me. And I finish off with the part about Star giving me the evil eye.

When I finally stop talking, the first words out of Alicia's mouth are: "Star Simons has always been a two-faced little witch."

I love Alicia.

"You should have seen her," I continue. "Anybody looking on—and people were watching us for sure—would swear she was being totally cool to me."

"I had Star in Spanish last year. Señor Marquez loved her. He thought she was the best thing since sliced tortillas. Neither of them appreciated my rapier wit. She used to give me these evil glares all the time. I know exactly what you're talking about. I wanted to push her face in."

I picture Alicia like she was in fourth grade, standing up

to those bullies. "Well, I get the feeling Star would like to push *my* face in, and I haven't even done anything."

"But you'd like to, right?"

I sigh into the phone for my answer.

"Well, you be careful, Mary Jane. She may look all girl, but I guarantee she'd fight dirty. And she wouldn't be alone. That girl would have backup."

I have never been in a fight. "Fight? Come on. The closest I've ever come to fighting was that time in elementary school with you, when we faced off those bullies." I laugh, but I can tell she's totally serious. We've seen plenty of girl-on-girl fights at Attila Ill. "Seriously, I'm not going to fight her, Alicia."

"Yeah. Well, just make sure *she* doesn't fight *you*."

"So what am I supposed to do? Stay away from Jackson?"

Alicia is quiet, like she's thinking it over. "I don't know what to tell you, kid. A month ago, I would have said no guy is worth fighting for. Now, well, Colt's changed everything. I'd fight a skyful of Stars for him."

Now it's my turn to be quiet. This is an Alicia I don't know. The old Alicia didn't believe in love. She admired what Red and Alex had but considered it the exception that proved her no-love rule.

"Hey, listen," Alicia says, her voice changing, softening. "Colt just walked in. I gotta jet. Keep me posted, okay?"

"Sure. Thanks, Alicia."

I hang up, and I'm more confused than ever. Alicia belongs to another world. I need help in this world, high school.

Like it or not, I'm stuck here for seven more months. I need to talk to Cassie.

Cassie picks up on the second ring. "Hello?" I don't think she has caller ID, because this is Cassie's deep and raspy voice, the one she uses on guys.

"Just me, Cassie," I say.

"Mary Jane! Man, I'm glad you called."

This expression of gladness doesn't make me feel better. Something's definitely wrong. "Why?" I ask suspiciously.

"I just finished IM-ing Nicole."

Not good. Somehow I know this. "And?"

"And she told me about you and Star."

"Me and Star?"

"Yeah. What went on with you guys in the hall today?" Cassie asks, making it sound like she's the district attorney, and I'm the one on trial.

"Nothing!" I protest. "Why? What did Nicole say happened?"

"She just said Star was upset by the things you said to her. I guess Nicole and Star and Lauren and some other kids were talking about it in that chat room they hang in."

I can't believe this. I'm getting run over on the information highway. I am Internet roadkill. "All I said to Star was what you guys told me to say. That I was sorry if she'd heard stuff about Jackson and me and that there wasn't anything to it."

"So why was she so upset?" Cassie asks.

"She wasn't! Not when she left. She waved and said

good-bye like we were buddies." I'm not sure why I don't add the part about the evil Star threatening me. But I don't think Cassie would believe it anyway.

"You should call Nicole and straighten this whole mess out, Mary Jane. She has to go pick up her little stepbrother in Cissna Park. She'll have her cell with her."

I hang up and dial Nicole. It rings four times before she answers. "What?"

"Nicole? This is Mary Jane."

"Oh." She doesn't exactly sound pleased to hear from me. "What do you want?"

"I want to straighten out this whole mess with Star."

"It's a little late for that, don't you think?"

"Late?"

"After the things you said to Star, I wouldn't blame her if she never forgave you." A horn blares in the background.

"Things I said to her? What did I say?"

"That you like Jackson. That you'll do whatever you want with her boyfriend. That—"

"I didn't say any of that!" I shout. "Did Star say I said those things?"

"You know what you said, Mary Jane," Nicole says coolly.

"I do know. And you don't. Because Star's lying. And Jackson and I don't have anything going. We joked around at Cassie's. Big deal! And *he* came and sat by me in English. Double big deal. So if Star's threatened by that, then she's in bad shape in the self-confidence department."

"You left the party together."

"For *four* minutes!" I protest.

Nicole breathes heavily into the phone. Then silence. Finally she asks, "Mary Jane, swear to me that you and Jackson aren't, like, going behind Star's back."

"Fine. I swear on a stack of pizzas, Nicole. Jackson barely knows I exist. He probably doesn't even—" I stop. My phone's cutting out, signaling an incoming call. "Hang on a minute, Nicole. I'm getting a call."

I put her on hold and take the other call. "Hello?"

"Hey." The voice on the other end is deep, strong, powerful. "Mary Jane?"

I can't answer. I know this voice.

"Mary Jane, this is Jackson."

10

Jackson!

"*Mary Jane?*"

It's Jackson 's voice. He's calling my name. So this could be a dream.

"Are you there?"

But in my dreams, he never asks if I'm there. They are, after all, *my* dreams.

"Is anybody there?"

I squeeze the phone.

"Hello?" he tries.

Jackson House called me on the phone. That means he took the time to look up my number. I imagine the scene, the man's persistence, as he pages through the *A*s, the *B*s, the Cs . . . Maybe he writes down my number when he finds it, the touch of the pencil reminding him of his pencil gift to me. He had to punch in every single digit to dial. Was he thinking of *me* the whole time?

"Mary J—oh, well. Weird."

He's hanging up! He's leaving! "Wait!" I shout into the phone.

"Mary Jane?"

"Yeah. I mean, hello."

"This is Jackson."

"Jackson."

"Jackson House . . . from good ol' Attila Ill?"

"Attila Ill." It seems all I can do is repeat his words. I have none of my own.

"Okay. So . . ."

I know it's my turn to speak. The voices in my head are all screaming at me, but their words clash into each other so I can't get a single word to come out.

"You still there?" Jackson asks.

You are blowing it! ***M.J.*** cries. *Tell him you were hoping he'd call.*

It's got to be a wrong number, ***Plain Jane*** insists. *Or maybe a prank? A crank call, with the entire football team listening in? But at least* he *called* you. *Be polite. Tell him you're on the other line.*

I'm on the other line! I totally forgot about Nicole.

"Jackson," I say, clearing my throat because my voice sounds wrinkled, "could you . . . would you . . . hold?"

"Hold?" He laughs, softly, manly. "Hold who?"

I can't breathe, but I manage to say, "The phone?"

"Oh, that." He sounds disappointed. I've disappointed Jackson House. "Okay."

My fingers shake so much I can hardly punch the line back to Nicole. When I do, she's hot.

"Hey! You're using up my minutes. I'm already way over. My rents are going to kill me."

"Sorry, Nicole."

"Who was it?"

For one terrifying second, I think this is a trap. She and Star have somehow gotten Jackson to phone me at this exact moment. It's a test. Will I or won't I come clean?

But I don't think Nicole is that smart.

"Nobody. Just homework stuff. Sorry."

"So where were we anyway?" Nicole asks.

I try to remember. Something about Star. I could care less. All I want to do is get back to Jackson. "Just tell Star there's nothing to be upset about, okay? See you Monday."

"Hold on!" Nicole shouts. "I didn't wait fifteen minutes so you could say two words. I'll need more than this to go back to Star. I'm over my minutes anyway. A few more won't matter. Star thinks you . . ."

I tune her out because I'm picturing Jackson tapping his foot, waiting for me to come back on the line.

". . . more than fair, if you ask me. So are you?"

There's a pause, and I realize Nicole has been talking and now expects some kind of answer from me. Why can't my split personalities kick in when I need them? I could let ***Plain Jane*** handle Nicole, and ***M.J.*** could get back to Jackson.

I take a stab. "You're right, Nicole. Whatever you say."

"Mary Jane, what's with you? You're, like, not there."

I raise my voice, going for righteous indignation. "Well, what do you expect, Nicole? All of a sudden, everybody in the whole school has turned against me! And for no reason, no matter what Star thinks."

"You're not blaming Star, are you?" Nicole accuses.

"Why is anybody blaming anybody?" I demand. "This whole inquisition is so out of order! Nothing's gone on! Nothing's going on!"

I can't stand it another second. Jackson has probably given up on me and hung up. He'll never call again. He'll never speak to me again. "Nicole, I have to go."

"Don't you hang up on me!" Nicole threatens.

"No, no, no. I'll be right back. Hang on."

I punch Nicole on hold, harder than I need to, and go back to Jackson.

"Jackson, are you still there?" I hold my breath. I will die right here, under my black ceiling, if he's gone.

"What? Oh, 'scuse me. I fell asleep."

"I'm so sorry. We're eating up your cell minutes and everything."

"Not really. I'm on the phone in my bedroom."

M.J.: *Did he just say "my bedroom"?*

I fight off the X-rated image forming in my head.

"You still there, Mary Jane?"

"Yes! I'm here, in *my* bedroom."

Plain Jane: *Don't say "bedroom"! What's wrong with you?*

He laughs. "Listen, Mary Jane. I just wanted to call and make sure you're okay."

"Okay?" I'm repeating again.

"Yeah. I know there's some crazy talk going around at school."

"Crazy talk?" I have to stop this.

"About you. And actually, about me." He sighs into the phone. I think I feel his breath.

"Yeah. About you and me," I say, trying not to repeat exactly.

"Anyway, you probably know that Star and I have been having problems for a long time."

I resist the urge to break out into the "Hallelujah Chorus." Jackson and Star have been having problems! And no wonder, since she's dating other guys behind his back.

"I know Star and her friends can be pretty protective," he continues, as if he can't hear me jumping on my bed. "I just don't want you to get hurt or anything."

"Thanks," I say, collapsing back onto my bed. Jackson House doesn't want me to get hurt. He is the nicest human on the face of the earth.

"Are you okay, then?" he asks.

I'm tearing up. "I'm okay," I squeak.

A tiny light flashes on the black of my ceiling. I realize

it's the phone light blinking, reminding me that Nicole is still on hold.

I have to get rid of her. "Could you hang on for just one second?" I don't let him answer because I couldn't stand it if he said no.

I punch buttons. "Hey. I'm really sorry about that. So, you can talk to Star?"

"What?" But it's Jackson's voice. "What do you mean?"

I'm still on with Jackson! "Nothing! Sorry. I'll be right back."

I punch buttons again. "Nicole?"

"This is getting really old, Mary Jane. And now my bratty stepbrother's with me. Just promise me that you and Jackson aren't talking."

"What?" It *is* a trap! She knows he's talking to me on the other line!

"Or seeing each other or anything," she adds.

I pull myself together. "Give me a break, Nicole," I plead.

"I'll do what I can," Nicole promises.

I'm aching to go back to Jackson. "Thanks. See you in school tomorrow!"

"Tomorrow's Saturday, Mary Jane," she explains.

"Okie doke." I don't think I've ever said "okie doke" in my whole life, and even in my confused state, I promise myself that I'll never say it again. "Bye." I press the button before she has a chance to start anything else.

"Hi again," I say, pulling out my sexy ***M.J.*** voice. "Sorry about that. I had to get rid of somebody."

"What?" It's Nicole. I've done it again, pressed the wrong button. Somebody should commit me.

I think fast. "Uh—I had to get rid of my mom?" I clear my throat as a possible explanation for the low, sexy voice. "So now we can say good-bye. Mom's gone. So bye, Nicole."

"Whatever," Nicole says. And she hangs up.

That leaves me alone with Jackson House. There is nowhere else on earth I'd rather be.

"Okay. I'm here. All yours." As soon as I say it, ***Plain Jane*** calls me *slut*. But I don't care. "Sorry that took so long."

"Me, too," Jackson says. "Now *I've* got to run."

"Nuh-uh," I say, sounding five years old. But it feels like he's leaving forever, going overseas to fight in an unjust war and die for love and country.

"'Fraid so," he says bravely. "I'm glad you're not taking the gossip to heart." There's a pause. "We did have fun at Cassie's, though. I guess I'd never seen that side of you before."

"What side?" I want to be sure I fully display the right side from now on. Lately, I've had more sides than an octagon.

He laughs, and I tumble into the sound of it. "I don't know," he begins. "Weird that we've gone to the same schools and never gotten to know each other until now."

"Yeah. Weird." But the words repeating in my brain are "*. . . until now . . . until now.*" They're right up there with "See ya."

11

Stallions

When Jackson and I disconnect, I plop back on my bed and stare up at the black ceiling. Even it can't spoil my mood. The ceiling is filled with images of Jackson, including imagined ones of Jackson and me. I replay every word of our conversation—editing out Nicole's interruptions—and search for deeper meaning in all of his words. I have to fight the urge to go over all the things I *should* have said. I must believe that I'll have another chance to say them. Soon.

The rents return and leave Sandy in my care so they can go out "on a date." They do this more Friday nights than I would ever admit to my friends. It's embarrassing to know that my rents have a more active dating life than I do.

I pop popcorn, and Sandy and I settle in to watch the *Scooby-Doo* movie for the eighty-seventh time. I don't mind because I'm not seeing the oversized dog or the characters who never change their clothes. I'm still playing my own little Jackson House movie in my head.

The phone rings, and I leap off the couch to answer it. My foot catches on the arm of the couch, and I fall on my face. Popcorn flies.

"Marwyjan! You okay?" Sandy runs over to scrape me off the floor.

"The phone!" I whisper, because the wind was knocked out of me. "Get the phone!" I'm imagining Jackson on the other end of the phone, waiting again.

Sandy wants to stay with me, but I shove her toward the still-ringing phone. She answers it. "Hello?"

I get to my knees and concentrate on getting my breath back.

"Yes," Sandy says to the phone. Without taking the phone from her lips, she turns to me and shouts, "It's a boy!"

Still on all fours, I reach out for her to give me the phone. She doesn't. "Marwyjan? She's my sister."

"Bring me the phone, Sandy!" I cry. My wind has nearly returned, but I'm still shaken. I sit where I am, on the floor, on top of the popcorn kernels. "Give me the phone!"

"She spilled her popcorn," Sandy's telling the phone.

"Sandy!" I shout.

"You can talk to her." She starts over to the couch but still has the receiver to her ear. "We're watching 'Scooby-Dooby-Doo, where are you?'" She sings this part.

When she's close enough, I grab the phone out of her hand. "Hello?" I've forgotten to use my sexy voice, so I say it again, "Hello?"

"Mary Jane?" It's a boy. But it's not Jackson.

"Yeah?" I kind of snap at the guy on the other end because he's not Jackson. And now I realize that my chin hurts. My left elbow and knee have rug burns.

"It's Brad." He waits, as if anticipating applause, doesn't get it, and goes on. "So, had any good pizza lately?"

I can't figure out why he'd call me. "Not really." I want to ask him why he's calling. Then I have a thought. Maybe he's calling for Jackson. Why else would he call me, when he's never even nodded at me in the halls?

"So . . ." He coughs, and it sounds fake, a nervous cough. "When are you coming out for the team? We can hold tryouts just for you. Say the word." He laughs, and it's as fake as his cough.

I want to cut to the chase, to make him admit that Jackson put him up to calling me, that Jackson wanted him to ask . . . ask what? What if I'm wrong? And even if I'm right, I have to play it cool. "I'm there, soon as you get those new outfits," I say, going for light and witty, and sexy and confident. "I suggest sienna. Goes great with my eyes."

"You got it," he jokes.

I can't stand this much longer. Sandy is glued to the

TV. I'm sitting in popcorn. "What can I do for you, Brad?" I ask.

That's my girl! ***M.J.*** cries. *Take control! Take charge!*

Two boys call you in one night? ***Plain Jane*** is highly suspicious. *Now I know this is all one big prank. Besides, isn't Brad going with Colleen?*

"I was thinking," Brad begins, "maybe we could get together tomorrow night."

I'm blown away. "You . . . and me?"

"Yeah."

He's not calling for Jackson. Brad is calling for himself. "Don't you have a game tomorrow night?" I ask, because it's the first thing I can think of. And it's lame. Guys go out after the game.

"Yeah," Brad says. "And then I kind of . . . well, I kind of made plans already for right after the game."

Told you so! ***Plain Jane***'s screaming. *He's got a date with Colleen already! So why is he asking you for a date when he's dating Colleen?*

Good question.

"Let me get this straight, Brad," I begin. "You already have a date after the game, right?"

"But I could take her home fast after that," he says quickly. "Then you and I could get together."

"Get together," I repeat, hoping this isn't what it sounds like.

"Yeah!"

"After your real date," I add, as the picture comes into focus and that cold-pizza-sauce feeling returns with a vengeance to the pit of my stomach.

"Yeah!" Brad sounds thrilled that I get it. His grand plan.

"And let me guess. This would be our little secret, right?" I'm praying that he'll say "Wrong!" That he'll be outraged that I've so grossly misunderstood his intentions.

"Right!" he says gleefully.

"Wrong!" I hang up on Brad, so hard the phone rattles.

This can't be happening. Not to me.

Did he really think I'd agree to . . . to . . . to what? He couldn't be thinking what I think he's thinking. But I'm not stupid. I watch MTV. I know what some girls do in cars when they disappear from parties. Could he really think . . . ? Is that possible? How could seventeen years of my reputation get tossed out for a mythical missing *four minutes?* How could that happen? To me? Mary Jane Ettermeyer! Member in good standing of Abstinence in Action!

I can't decide whether to cry, to throw things, or to throw up. Or maybe I should enter the Witness Protection Program and start life over.

Before I can make up my mind, the phone rings again.

"What?" I say when I pick up the receiver. I'm expecting it to be Brad again, asking why I hung up on him.

"Mary Jane?" It's a male voice. But it's not Brad. And it's not Jackson.

"This is Mary Jane," I admit cautiously.

"Sweet! This is Tim."

Tim is even worse at small talk than Brad was. And I have even less patience for it. Once again, I'm picturing my name and number scrawled on bathroom walls.

He finally gets around to popping his big question. "Wanna go out and do something?"

Inside, I feel myself drowning in a pool of thick red pizza sauce. But I keep telling myself that none of this is my fault, and I haven't done anything drowning-worthy and I will not let them hear me cry. I swallow hard and brace myself for a performance that would make Nicole jealous.

"Tempting, Tim," I say, gathering all my ***M.J.*** forces to muster an iota of sarcasm.

"Cool."

I should have known sarcasm would disappear into the black hole of Tim's mind. "I can't. I'm watching Sandy while my folks are gone."

"Sweet! So can I come over?" Tim asks. "Your parents aren't home, right?"

I cannot keep this stiff-upper-lip routine going one more second. "I'm hanging up now, Tim."

He's saying something, but I can't make it out as the phone clicks off.

How did this happen? It's like the ozone layer finally caved, and the carbon monoxide's driven everybody stark raving mad.

I pick up the spilled popcorn, then plop onto the couch next to Sandy, just as the *Scooby-Doo* credits roll. We watch one of Sandy's shows on Nickelodeon. Then I make her take a bath while I clean up the kitchen.

While Sandy's in the bath, I get two more calls. One from Michael, who's in my psych class. And one from Tyler, who plays ball with Brad. I know for a fact that Tyler's been going with Emma Phillips for almost a year. I think I'm getting an ulcer.

And the voices inside my head are ganging up on me:

Plain Jane: *You've really done it this time. You have to get your parents to move. There's no way you can continue going to Attila High. You should have seen this coming!*

M.J.: *What's the big deal? Guys want you! It doesn't mean you have to give them what they want. They want you! This is what you've always dreamed of. You go, girl!*

Sandy huddles under the covers in her purple flannel jammies, and I pull the cowgirl blanket up to her chin. Her whole room is covered in horse—horse posters, horse lamp, horse calendar, horse bedspread. She even has a real saddle on a sawhorse in the corner of the room. The only thing missing is a real horse, which is what she wants more than anything in the world. When I'm on my own, I plan to live on a farm just so I can get Sandy a horse and keep it for her.

"Tell me a story," she says. It's the command every night when I'm on duty. When we were little and shared a room, she'd make me tell her a story every night. She likes books read to her, but she'd rather have me make up stories that she can help with.

"Okay. But then you have to promise to go right to sleep." I begin with "Once upon a time . . ." because if I don't, she stops me and makes me start over:

"Once upon a time, there were four horses that lived out in the wilderness. And their names were . . ." I stop, like I always do, and look to Sandy.

"Jerry. And . . . Jacob. And Jeff and Jimmy," Sandy supplies. As often as we've told the story, I don't think she's ever given any horses the same name.

"All boys, huh?" I ask.

"Stallions," she corrects.

"Right. Well, Jerry and Jacob and Jeff and Jimmy lived in a valley between two mountain peaks. They got along fine. But one day, Jeff said, 'I wish we could meet some more horses.' And Jerry said, 'Let's all wish the same thing. Then maybe it will happen.' "

Fortunately, Sandy isn't picky about plotlines. All she really waits for is the chance to name the horses.

"So they all wished together, in a giant horse wish, that they could meet more horses. And the next day, four pure white horses came trotting along. 'Man . . . I mean, stallion, are we glad to see you!' Jerry exclaimed. 'What are your names?' And one by one, the white horses answered." I look to Sandy again.

" 'I'm Max,' " Sandy says, in this cute, horsy voice she has. " 'And I'm Mick.' 'I'm Mark.' 'And I'm Michael.' "

"All guys—I mean stallions—again, Sandy?" I ask. I don't want her to grow up thinking it's a man's world, so I try again. "But in the valley below, a brown horse was kicking up *her* heels, her hooves, and whinnying. And when the stallions saw her horsing around, they all started galloping down to meet her." I stop, picturing the brown horse raising her head, as the stallions careen down the hill after her.

"Go on!" Sandy demands. "What happens to the brown mare?"

The phone rings. I pick up Sandy's purple phone. "Hello?"

"Hey, Mary Jane?" says the caller. "This is Colby Paxton. I'm in your English class. I wondered if you want to go out sometime."

I close my eyes and picture those stallions racing faster and faster down the hill.

And suddenly, I know exactly how that mare feels.

12

The Twisted Pretzel

Saturday morning I drive to Springmill Mall and park Fred in the back lot. I wear a scarlet letter *F* for "Flirt" on my sweater. Not really. But I'm trying to stop obsessing over my stupid reputation and regain my innate, though buried, sense of humor.

I know I will need said sense of humor this morning. Since August, I've worked most Saturdays and some Friday nights and Sundays at The Twisted Pretzel. This is not a job I want to spend the rest of my life doing, but it's better than my last two jobs. Last summer I stuffed fliers in ad rags and delivered them—until I got fired because they actually wanted me to get there at seven. In the morning. In the summer.

Before that, I had a job walking dogs. But I only did it for two days. Dogs are not really our best friends, it turns out.

Luckily, The Twisted Pretzel is in the far corner of the mall, by Ritz Department Store and Fine China, where few high school kids venture. Our sign promises fifty varieties of pretzel, but I've never sold more than a dozen. I used to like pretzels before I worked here.

There are several things about my job, besides the minimum wage, that would keep me from pursuing a career in pretzels:

• I have to wear a white hat in the shape of a triangle that says THE TWISTED PRETZEL on it. No amount of begging can make my boss change this rule.

• My boss. Peter Pretzel (real name, Peter Prater) is a little man who believes he is in a position of power, where he no doubt has never been before. Someday I intend to introduce him to Ms. Lake, the school librarian/serial ax murderer. It's not that I necessarily want him to be her next victim. I'd just like to see her shush him.

• Plastic gloves, which would be a better fit on my feet.

• Robbie, my coworker. Actually, Robbie is a sweet kid, a pimply freshman, who asks me out every day after work.

We coexist in a six-by-six, linoleum-floored cubicle, with a glass counter in front and a silver oven in back.

"You're late," Pretzel Boss grumbles as I slip behind the counter and don my charming white hat.

I don't point out that in the scope of time eternal, five minutes is hardly late. The man has no depth.

Robbie comes up and whispers, "I tried to cover for you."

I raise eyebrows at Robbie. "How'd you do that? Tell him I'm actually here, but he can't see me?" I pull on the plastic gloves and raise my voice for my Pretzel Boss. "Sorry, boss. Won't happen again."

"It better not," he warns.

I mouth the words as he says them because Pretzel Bosses are so predictable.

"You look nice today," Robbie says, staring at me like he always does. I don't think Robbie has heard the current Mary Jane rumors. This is simply his way of relating. He's a head shorter than I am, so he's eye level with my boobs, which works out well for the boy, since that's exactly where he's constantly looking.

"Thanks, Robbie. Go away now."

Mall traffic has picked up every week since October. Now that we're done with Halloween, it's worse than ever. Christmas decorations have taken over at the mall, as if nobody could wait for Thanksgiving to be over with. Alicia and I used to write letters to Congresspersons, demanding a law against celebrating Christmas before Thanksgiving was over. We only heard back from one lawmaker. He told us how cute we were for writing, and he ended his letter, dated November 15, with "Merry Christmas." Alicia and I promised that when we could vote, in about eight years, we'd never vote for him.

Pretzel Boss pulls out two Santa hats, floppy red numbers with the white ball tassel on the end. "I got these for you two. You can start wearing them next weekend."

I consider telling him about my moral stand on Christmas-before-Thanksgiving, but he's already mad at me for being late.

"Cool!" Robbie exclaims. "So we'll be, like, Mr. and Mrs. Claus!"

"Never going to happen, Robbie my boy," I whisper, after Pretzel Boss moves out of hearing range.

I'm not sure how much longer I can work here anyway. The rents will shower me with disappointment if I lose another job. But I refuse to work the Friday after Thanksgiving, commonly referred to in the mall biz as THE shopping day. I won't miss Sandy's big game. And that's that. I haven't asked for the day off yet because I'm pretty sure the only reason Pretzel Boss is keeping me on is that he needs me for THE shopping day of the year. If he can't have me then, I think he'll fire me on the spot.

As I take my turn twisting pretzels and sticking trays into the oven, I'm thinking that getting fired on the spot is looking better and better. Maybe I should tell Pretzel Boss right now that I refuse to work on THE day. Might as well get it over with and be rid of this job. Plus, I could tell the rents I did it for my sister Sandy.

On the other hand, maybe I shouldn't get fired yet.

Plain Jane: *Of course you can't quit! What were you thinking? You are so lucky to have a job in a nice, warm mall, when millions of people all over the world are jobless and homeless.*

On the other hand, you should see yourself in that hat!

M.J. (who habitually kicks into whine mode the minute I step behind The Twisted Pretzel counter): *Pretzels are embarrassing. It would be so much cooler if you'd get a job at Abercrombie. Or Hollister. Even the Gap or Banana Republic. Or Bebe! Then your friends would drop in to see you and use your discount!*

Life is too short to wear a white triangle hat and twist pretzels.

The first hour we're open is busier than I've ever seen it. All that shopping must make shoppers hungry. They order things like the Egg Pretzel, Bacon-and-Pretzel, and Cinnamon Swirl, with frosting.

"My turn to bake," Robbie says, which means I have to take a turn at the counter.

People who do Christmas shopping apparently don't believe in the Christmas spirit. And whoever claimed that the customer is always right certainly never worked at The Twisted Pretzel.

I pull on a fresh, clean pair of my fashionable transparent gloves and prepare to meet the public in my equally fashionable hat. For the next twenty minutes, it's all I can do to keep our line down to six, which is our unofficial magic number for survival.

Then all of a sudden, there's nobody. This is the way it always works. It's almost like the customers huddle around the corner until their numbers increase past six, then rush the counter, like we're in the Great Depression, and this is the free breadline. Somebody then sounds a silent whistle, and they magically disappear . . . until the next onslaught.

I take advantage of the down time to sprinkle candies on the Sweet-Treat Pretzels and peppermint on the Peppermint Pretzels. If I had to do this during rush hour, I would run the risk of being bodily assaulted by a whacked-out bargain hunter who believed my menial task was keeping her from getting the buy of the century.

I'm shaking those tasteless, multicolored candies onto pretzels when I hear the *chink, chink, chink* of a customer's keys on the glass pretzel case. It's a familiar sound, used by customers everywhere to get the peasants' attention. I have half a mind to pretend I don't get it.

Again comes the sound of keys rattling glass.

"May I help you?" I ask, in a tone that won't win me any Employee of the Month awards. I look up at the offending customer.

But what I see are the big brown eyes of Jackson House.

Instinctively, I pull off my white hat, forgetting that I've pinned it in place with bobby pins. Pins and hair now stick up, and I slap at them with my plastic gloves.

"Hat, Mary Jane!" Pretzel Boss yells. "You want to get me shut down?"

I do. But I don't have time to get into it now.

I replace my hat and move to the counter. A woman with at least fourteen shopping bags takes a spot behind Jackson.

"So, what's good here?" Jackson asks, all kindness and full

of niceness, as if I weren't standing before him in plastic gloves and a triangular hat.

"Do you really want a pretzel?" I ask.

"Don't take this the wrong way, Mary Jane," he says, "but I think your salesmanship could use a little work."

The woman behind him clears her throat, as if in agreement.

I think I'm smiling, but the voices in my head are making it impossible for me to speak:

Plain Jane: *I repeat: Have you seen yourself in that hat? This guy is here for a pretzel. Not for you, you idiot. The line is growing. You're up to six people now.*

M.J.: *Jackson House is so into you! He came to the mall just to see who? YOU! Forget this job. Jump over this counter and into his arms!*

Jackson reaches into the pocket of his letter jacket and comes out with his wallet. "Guess you better give me a pretzel before the line stampedes me."

"Which one?" I ask. "I mean, which pretzel?"

"Your pick."

"You sure?" I ask, reaching into the case of pretzels.

"Hey, I trust you, Mary Jane."

"Yeah? You're the only one at Attila Ill who does."

"That bad, huh?" he asks. "Is it my fault?"

The question surprises me. Is it? Is all of this Jackson's

fault? I can't believe I never asked myself this question. I know what locker-room talk is. Was I the topic of conversation in the Attila Ill locker room? I don't want to believe *my* Jackson House would do a thing like that. Lie. Spread rumors about me to beef up his guy-rep. But he and I are the only two people on earth who know what happened when we left Cassie's together, that *nothing* happened. He could have made up anything.

"Did you say something about me?" I demand. "Like to the guys at school?" My heart is thumping, and the blood racing through my veins makes me short of breath.

The shopping-bag woman behind Jackson leans forward, listening, frowning.

And I discover I'm angry. At her. And at him. "Well? Did you?"

"What are you talking about?" he asks, brow furrowed.

"Do I have to spell it out?" I snap.

His head jerks back as if I've slapped him. "No. If you're asking me if I made up something about you, Mary Jane, the answer is no."

The blood coursing through my veins comes to an abrupt stop. He's hurt. I have hurt Jackson House.

"I wouldn't do that," he continues, calmly, softly, "especially to you, Mary Jane."

"Especially to me?" I repeat.

The corners of his lips turn up slightly. "I admire you too much."

"You do? Admire *me?*" I know. I'm in repeat mode again, but I can't help myself. I can't take my eyes off his eyes, his soft, brown, totally truth-telling eyes.

"Hurry it up, will you?" shouts the mad shopper, who obviously considers the show over.

Jackson smiles down at me. "Could I have my pretzel, ma'am?"

I give him my warmest, most admirable smile and select the biggest pretzel from the case, hoping he will accept these gestures as my apology. How could I ever have doubted this man? "I'm giving you our specialty Popcorn Pretzel," I explain.

"Which would explain the popcorn kernels all over it," he observes. "How did you stick them on there?"

"Don't ask." I place the bumpy pretzel on a wrapper and present it to Jackson. "Specialty of the house." Forever after, I will call it "The Jackson House," at least in my head.

"Perfect," he says. "Popcorn, in honor of our first night together." He winks.

I blush, which I know because my cheeks feel hotter than the pretzel oven.

When he takes the pretzel from me, his fingers touch my plastic-wrapped fingers and linger way longer than necessary for the pretzel exchange.

He did that on purpose! **M.J.** screams.

Nuh-uh. You're such a klutz. He was probably afraid you'd drop the thing, **Plain Jane** insists.

The woman behind Jackson makes a noise that sounds like "Harrumph."

The line is a dozen people long.

"What do I owe you for this masterpiece?" Jackson asks, grinning, showing a dimple.

"Owe me?" Our fingers are still touching.

"Problem, Mary Jane?" Pretzel Boss asks, looking over my shoulder. His breath smells like the Fire-Eater's Red-Hot Pretzel.

I tell Jackson how much his pretzel costs, and he counts out the change exactly, forking it over in pennies, nickels, and dimes. I think he's taking his time on purpose. It's all I can do not to burst out laughing.

"There," he says, plopping down the final penny.

I slide the change into my palm. "Nice doing business with you, sir. Come again."

"Oh, I will," he promises. "See ya."

And I totally believe him.

13

Mall Matters

The rest of the morning, I keep making mistakes. I give the woman who orders the Elvis Pretzel the Lawrence Welk instead. I give the Chubby Checker Twist to a kid who asked for Chocolate Dream.

My heart isn't in my work . . . because it's with Jackson House.

"You better let me wait on customers," Robbie says after I mess up three orders in a row.

But I turn out to be as lousy making the pretzels as I was serving them. I put salt on the Sweet Cinnamon Pretzel and red hots in the Tangerine Twist. Since the pretzels have to be thrown out, Pretzel Boss bans me from kitchen duty, and I end up back behind the counter.

"Mary Jane!" Cassie calls. She's wearing her new knee-high boots with a leather skirt. No triangle hat. She walks up to the front, ignoring the glares from real customers. "When do you get off?"

"Five!" I shout over to her.

"When you're done, meet me at Mahoney's!" she shouts back.

I nod, and she waves and walks off. Sometimes, if we're both dateless, we meet at the mall and get a hamburger at Mahoney's, then check out the movies or go to the game together. If Cassie knew Jackson's fingers had been touching mine, she'd never invite me to anything again.

I'm counting the minutes until five o'clock when I glance down the line and see Jackson House at the very end of the line.

I process orders faster than any server has ever processed orders at The Twisted Pretzel. Finally, I call the next customer with "Next." And it's Jackson.

He stands in front of me, on the other side of the counter. Smiling, dimpling, if there is such a word.

Pretzel Boss stops what he's doing and frowns at us.

"Do you have any pretzels?" Jackson asks, without a trace of amusement.

"Yes, we do," I answer, equally serious.

"That's great!" he exclaims, as if I've just informed him we're running a special on the secret to life.

"What kind of pretzel do you want?" I ask, using every ounce of willpower to keep this looking serious, professional.

He scratches his chin and narrows his brown eyes. "Well, what kinds of pretzels do you have?" He waits for my answer.

So I begin. "Apple Pretzel, A La Mode Pretzel, Blueberry Pretzel, Berry Berry Pretzel, Candy-Coated Pretzel, Charlie Chaplin Pretzel, Chocolate Dream Pretzel, Chubby Checker Twist Pretzel, Davy Crockett Pretzel, Elvis Pretzel . . ." And I keep going until I've listed all fifty varieties, as the line grows and grows.

"I believe I'll take the regular pretzel with salt," Jackson says when I'm all done.

I give him the pretzel, and he leaves.

But an hour later he's back for more. The crowd has thinned, and Robbie and I are both waiting on customers until we need to bake more pretzels.

This time Jackson chooses the Romeo, a handsome garlic pretzel with red hearts all over it. As far as I know, nobody has ever ordered it before.

"You must really love pretzels," Robbie observes, ringing up the Romeo.

Instead of directing his answer at Robbie, Jackson turns to me with a long, slow smile. "Nope. I hate the things. Never touch 'em."

Finally, the clock admits it's five o'clock. I whip off my hat and gloves and try to smooth down my hair. Then I grab my coat off the rack in back. "When are you going home, Robbie?" I ask.

"Closing. I need the extra hours."

"Well, thanks for covering for me today. I know I was even worse than usual."

Robbie inches toward me, his eyes big as Ping-Pong balls, looking where they always look. "Mary Jane, do you want to go out with me after closing?"

I smile down on him. "Not going to happen, Robbie. But thanks anyway." You have to hand it to the kid for persistence.

I make a pit stop, brush my hair, apply lipstick, and head out to Mahoney's. I would rather go straight home and lie on my bed, stare at the black ceiling, and dream of Jackson House. But I promised Cassie I'd meet her. I'll just hope I can act normal. As I've thought so many times before, it was very smart of God not to let us read one another's minds. If we could read other people's thoughts, I'll bet nobody would have friends.

I round the corner to Mahoney's and stop. Cassie's sitting at a table out front. And with her are Samantha, Nicole . . .

And Star.

At first, ***Plain Jane*** is so overcome that she doesn't know what to say about this new development. So she falls back on the old standbys: *Your hair looks horrible. You're wearing the wrong clothes. You're fat*. Then Star looks directly at me with a glare that would terrify an ax murderer. *Flee the building!* ***Plain Jane*** shouts. *Step away from the mall!*

Forget that, **M.J.** reasons. *Who needs these girls? Why waste time with them when Jackson might still be around?*

Before I can decide which voice to listen to, Cassie stands up and waves me over.

I wave back weakly and start toward their table at a pace slightly under the speed of a glacier.

There's one empty chair at the table, next to Star. She's wearing khakis and a white shirt, unbuttoned to the legal limit. Her makeup is perfect, and her hair's been curled into long, flowing locks, suitable for a princess.

Instead of taking the empty seat, I greet everybody and escape to the serving counter, where I order a Diet Coke. This doesn't take very long, and I have to trudge back to the table and take the seat they've obviously set up for me.

"How was work?" Cassie asks.

The others are dead silent, even though they were laughing their heads off when I was on my Diet Coke mission.

"Just another day in the pretzel mines," I answer.

Nobody chuckles.

"Nice sweater, Mary Jane," Star says.

I'm almost sure she sneers as she says this. I'm wearing an ugly brown fuzz sweater that I'd only wear when I knew I'd be getting pretzel goo on me. My mother got it in a going-out-of-business sale, and it explains why that store was going out of business. This sweater is *not* nice.

I glance around the table, then back to Star. Her smirk is gone, and I know I was the only one who saw it.

"You've had that sweater for ages, haven't you?" Cassie comments. "I'll bet it's warm."

I try to smile at Cassie because I almost feel sorry for her. She's working hard to make this little reunion fly. It's obvious she's called us all together to patch things up. But this isn't how things work in high school, and Cassie should know that. Nothing's ever solved directly with girls. It's some kind of high school rule, I think. Problems are fixed through third parties. Someone calls on behalf of someone else, and then everybody pretends things are fine.

Maybe that's what we're doing now, pretending things are fine.

I want to come right out and ask if they've heard the four-minute rumor. I want to swear on a stack of French fries that the rumor is a big, fat, greasy lie. But what if they haven't heard it? What if the rumor never left the locker room guys? Then *I'd* be the one spreading it. It would be like gossiping about myself.

We're too quiet, so Cassie tries again. "Anyway, I need to get a job. I think it's great, Mary Jane, the way you hold down a job, keep up with school, babysit for your sister."

"I agree," Star says. "I guess it doesn't leave you much time for a dating life, huh?"

I feel her words like tiny arrows, barbed at the tip. But the other girls nod sympathetically, agreeing with her.

Man, she's good! **M.J.** exclaims, giving credit where credit is due. She vows that the brown sweater will go straight into the trash, never to be worn again.

Plain Jane is still obsessing over the fact that Mom bought that sweater out of the goodness of her heart and that it *is* very warm. Plus, the color matches my eyes.

I sip my Diet Coke and try to keep myself in on conversations that range from Sigh Fry to the sale at Music World, to taking our ACTs. We carefully stay away from guy-talk, which cuts our usual topic selection in half.

But as we sit here together, a strange thing happens. I relax. If these girls, The Girls, have heard stupid rumors about me, they obviously don't believe them. I start enjoying myself, enjoying my friends. My laughter is real, blending with theirs. When Cassie gossips about Trish, this girl we knew last year who dropped out of school, I'm really into it. And when Nicole rags on her little stepbrother, I feel sorry for both of them.

"Hey!" Cassie exclaims. "Why don't we all go to the game together? We can hang at my place afterwards."

"That'd be fun," I say, feeling almost like my old self again. It's embarrassing not to have a date to the game on a Saturday night. But there's strength in numbers. If we all went together, nobody would think we were losers.

"I've got a date," Star says as if she's apologizing.

"Me too," Nicole's quick to add.

"Wes is meeting me outside"—Samantha checks her watch—"in about five minutes."

"But you girls go and have fun," Star advises Cassie and me.

And I wonder if I'm the only one who hears the false pity in her voice.

What if I'm wrong about Star? I mean, what if I've imagined the sneer, the smirk, and the false pity? Could I really be imagining the tension between Star and me? *Objects may be closer than they appear.* And if I've imagined that, have I imagined everything, including Jackson and me?

I need answers. I want to know right now where Jackson and Star really stand. Jackson said they'd been having trouble. How much? What kind? What would Star say about their relationship? I have to know. And Star Simons is the only one who can tell me.

"Star," I begin, not sure how to phrase this.

"Hey! Hi, honey!" Star stands up and waves directly over my head as if she's flagging down a cab. She scoots back her chair and swoops around the table.

Coming toward us is Jackson House.

I am speechless. Breathless. Brainless.

Star throws herself at Jackson, hugging him and kissing his cheek.

"I thought you'd never get here!" Star says, slipping her arm around Jackson's waist and pulling him back to our table. They're dressed alike—khakis and white shirts.

Now I suspect that Cassie wasn't the one who set up this little reunion. This show is for my benefit. Star leads him right to where she was sitting, next to me.

Jackson smiles down at me, but it's not a better smile than he aims at Nicole and Cassie.

"We girls have had the best time!" Star exclaims. Smiling broadly, she leans back against the table. Her painted fingernails are spread out on the table, inches from me. Her perfume is strong.

She leans farther back, revealing that her unbuttoned white shirt may have exceeded the legal limit.

I see her fingers sliding toward my Diet Coke. Then, before I can get a sound out, her hand moves in a tiny sweeping motion.

"Don't!" I plead. My Coke glass wipes out. Diet Coke and ice spatter all over me. I feel it seeping into the brown fuzz and soaking my bra and stomach.

"Oh no!" Star cries. "Mary Jane, what did you do? Here. Let me help." She picks up napkins and dabs at my sweater.

I shove her hand away. "I've got it."

Cassie offers me a fistful of napkins.

I take them and try to soak up the syrupy mess.

"Well . . ." Star picks up her coat from her chair. "We've got to get going."

Nicole and Samantha stand up. "Me too," Nicole says.

"Have fun, guys," Samantha says to nobody in particular as she puts on her coat. She and Nicole walk off together.

Star hands her coat to Jackson, who helps her on with it. She pokes her arms through the sleeves, then turns to smile at him. Her back is to me, but her painted fingernails and the hand that spilled Diet Coke are just inches away.

Then, a nanosecond before she grabs Jackson's arm, Star's hand lifts in the air . . .

And she gives me the finger.

14

Bucker-Uppers

"*Did you see that?*" I demand of Cassie, when she finishes waving good-bye to our "friends."

"See what?" she asks, which pretty much gives me my answer.

"Star gave me the finger!"

Cassie smiles at me like I smile at Sandy sometimes. "Oh, Mary Jane, she did not."

"Yeah! She did!" But I can already see Cassie's not going to believe me, even if mall security caught it on tape and hands it over to us.

"You're just upset because you ruined your sweater and—"

"I didn't ruin my sweater!" I shout. People at other tables

turn and stare at us. At me. "Not that it would have mattered. I hate this sweater. But that was Star, too!"

Cassie gives a sigh worthy of Sigh Fry. "Admit it, Mary Jane. You're jealous of Star."

Duh, ***Plain Jane*** agrees.

Me? Jealous of that skinny, two-faced witch? **M.J.** challenges.

My soaked sweater is sticking to me, combining syrupy cola with fuzz and making me itch. "I'm going home," I say, grabbing my coat and making for the exit.

"But what about the game?" Cassie calls after me.

"Tell them they'll have to play without Mary Jane Ettermeyer!" I shout.

By the time I pull into the driveway, both Fred and I smell like rusty mothballs. My anger has morphed through the three or four stages of grief we had to read about in my psych class. Denial, anger, sadness, and I forget the others because I'm stuck deep in the middle of sadness.

I really thought Jackson liked me. I was so sure he and Star were history, an ugly blot on the timeline of the past. But there he was, hugging Star and barely glancing at me.

I hope he chokes on his pretzels.

The rents are waiting for me when I walk in. Mom's pixie nose turns up, and I know it's because I smell like the shaggy dog they'd never let me have for a pet when I was a kid.

She takes a step back. "Your brown sweater! What—? How—? I *loved* that sweater. Mary Jane, what happened to you?"

"Diet Coke," I answer.

"But . . . how . . . ?"

All I want to do is take a hot shower. And never come out. "Long story, and I'm beat. I'm just going to turn in early." I start to walk past them.

"Now? Tonight?" Dad asks. "Isn't there a game tonight?"

I'm surprised he's in tune enough to know this, but I nod. I find that it takes all my energy reserves to move my head up and down.

Mom takes over the interrogation. "So why are you staying home?"

I'm thinking I can't win. They were crazy when I came in late, and they're crazy when I'm early. Rents. "I have homework?" This is not a lie. It also has nothing to do with why I'm staying home.

I start to push past them again, but they're not done.

"Mary Jane," Mom says without looking at me, "we need to talk."

I'm getting the distinct feeling that there's more going on here than my cola-soaked sweater and an early Saturday night appearance. I don't know what's coming, but it's been the kind of day that could bring anything. I realize that I need to brace myself, to buck up. But there's nothing left in me but wet fuzz. I may be the daughter of the Queen of the Bucker-

Uppers, but I'm no princess. She didn't pass me that particular DNA. I wait.

"The phone's been ringing all day," Mom says.

Then I get it. The calls didn't stop just because I wasn't home. Stupid as it was, I guess I'd hoped it would all go away, that the rumor would be as dead as my relationship with Jackson House. "Sorry?" I say weakly.

"Living room," orders my dad, a man of few words, except when he's in court, which is what this is starting to feel like. "Now."

The three of us sit together in the living room, and I try to remember the last time we gathered like this. I think it was right after Alicia and I made crank calls to our neighbors accusing them of shoplifting, only they all recognized my voice and told my mother.

Dad begins for the prosecution. "Your mother says you've been receiving a large number of phone calls, all of them from boys. What do you know about this, Mary Jane?"

I don't know what to say, so I repeat. "A large number of phone calls? From boys?"

"A *very* large number of calls," Mom confirms. "All of them from boys."

I nod, taking in this information and buying time. I could make up something. I'm pretty sure I could get Dad to believe me. *It's a science experiment. It's our communications assignment.*

"Well?" My dad can say more in that one word than most people can in entire speeches.

Mom's sitting on the edge of her chair. "Something is very, very wrong here. I can feel it. Is there something you need to tell us, Mary Jane? Why are these boys calling you?"

This is beyond embarrassing. How do you tell your rents that every guy in the school is calling you to have sex? Probably. Or at least some form thereof. And if you do tell them, how do you convince them that the only reason guys think this is because of a measly missing four minutes?

Dad comes over and sits beside me on the couch. "Mary Jane, what is it? You can tell us." His voice is calm. It makes me want to confess, but there's nothing *to* confess. He should be a priest.

"I didn't do anything." But I can't look at them, so I doubt I'm believable. I stare at my hands as my fingers nervously pick brown fuzz from my sweater. "I swear. I haven't done anything wrong. They just think I did. Or will. Or would."

"Are we talking about slander, Mary Jane? Is someone spreading rumors about you to these boys?" My dad has turned back into Thomas Ettermeyer, Attorney at Law. I think he smells a lawsuit. "I want names."

Even if I wanted to supply this information, I can't. I believed Jackson when he said he hadn't made up anything to anyone about our *four minutes* together. Then again, I believed him when he said he and Star were as good as over.

"I don't have names, Dad," I plead.

I watch his face collapse. For an instant, he thought he could fix all this with a solid defamation of character suit.

But I think the reality is sinking in that even a class action against my class wouldn't help.

I'm starting to feel sorry for him.

"What *can* we do then, honey? Those boys can't just say things like that, can they? Can you tell your principal? We can't let them ruin your reputation." Mom appears to be a mascara-laden eyelash away from tears.

I glance from Mom to Dad and back. And I know it's up to me. This is my problem.

"Don't worry about this, okay?" I say, and my voice raises an octave. "I didn't do anything, and all I have to do now is tell kids the truth. It might take a couple of days. But everything will blow over. The truth will out." I rack my brain for more clichés. "This too shall pass." I realize I'm making about as much sense as my rents do when they attempt to advise me in matters of life and love. I feel as if I'm tossing peanuts to starving pigeons. But my rents *are* starving, and they're taking the pigeon feed. They're buying it because they need to. The carved channels in their faces are returning to lines.

"Really?" Mom asks.

I nod as if I'm positive. "Stuff like this happens all the time. Not to me," I add quickly. "It's probably over already. But you better let me field the calls this weekend, just in case. Anyway, there's nothing for you to worry about."

"I don't know, Mary Jane," Dad says. But he leans back and appears to be breathing normally again. "I could make some calls, file a complaint. . . ."

I manage a smile, an actual smile. "That would make things worse, Dad. Let me handle it, okay? Thanks for the concern. Seriously, I appreciate it. It was good to talk things out and all. And you'll be the first to know if I need a lawyer. But it's all going to be okay."

I get up from the couch and head for the stairs. They don't stop me. My rents have believed me. True, they've believed me because they wanted to, needed to. Rents have an irresistible need to believe that everything is hunky-dory (their words, not mine) with their kids. *I* don't believe me. I wish I did, but I don't. And yet I have just pulled off an amazing thing.

I have bucked up.

Mary Jane Ettermeyer may have gotten the Bucker-Upper gene after all.

15

Midnight Madness

I shower the Diet Coke off of me, put on my comfiest nightie, then lie on my bed and stare at the ceiling, fighting off images of Star and Jackson. In my mind, they turn into Barbie and Ken, then back again. I see them in their khakis and matching white shirts on the cover of *Teen Idols,* their back view on the back of the magazine, his arm around her waist, her thumb hooked in his belt loop.

The voice of ***M.J.*** in my head wishes Star's middle finger would get slammed in Jackson's car door. It wouldn't get broken, but Star would definitely have to wear a splint on it. And everyone would see the kind of girl she really is.

I must have fallen asleep, because I jerk myself awake to

the national anthem. It's the tune I picked for my cell. Besides the fact that nobody else has it, I figure if I leave my cell on in class and get a call, the teacher may be less likely to yell at a real patriot.

It's pitch dark in my room, so I have to grope for the phone. I pick up just as it's switching to voice mail. "Hello?" I sound like I have a mouth full of brown fuzz, which is exactly what my mouth feels like. I didn't brush my teeth before I fell asleep.

"Mary Jane, I'm sorry. Did I wake you up?"

The cobwebs in my head clear instantly, and I sit bolt upright. It's Jackson.

"Jackson? What time is it?" This is the least of the questions swirling in my head, but it's the first one to pop out.

"After midnight. I know. It's late. I just needed to talk to you."

"Talk to me?" Again with the repeating.

"Yeah. Can we talk?" He pauses. "Please, Mary Jane?"

"Why would I want to talk to you?" I demand.

"Because I'm asking you nicely," he answers.

I should hang up on him right now after all he's put me through.

"Because I won't sleep until you let me talk to you," he continues.

"Why would I believe a word you say?" I'm trying to stay totally angry with him. But I can't stop picturing his brown eyes red and bloodshot . . . because of me.

"I don't blame you for not wanting to hear me out," he

says. "But I'm asking you to anyway. Please? Five minutes. Give me five minutes?"

I listen for the voices in my head and wonder if they're still asleep.

"I'll do anything, Mary Jane," he pleads.

At the very least, I could hear him out, then demand that he call every boy in Attila Ill in a massive un-gossip campaign.

"Just five minutes?" he begs.

I sigh into the phone. I'll hear him out. What can it hurt? "Okay. You've got five minutes." I look at my watch, but it's too dark to see the minute hand.

"Great! I'm outside. Hurry, okay?" And he cuts off.

"Outside?" I reach behind me and pull back the curtain on my only bedroom window. Jackson's Jeep Cherokee is sitting under our half-bare maple tree. *He's outside!*

For a second I stay where I am. Then I grab my blue, wooly robe, step into the matching fuzzy slippers, and barrel downstairs at the speed of light, tying the robe's belt as I clear the last step. Only after I shut the front door behind me and take a hit from the icy wind do I hear the cacophony of voices in my head:

Plain Jane: *This is crazy, even for you! He made his girlfriend choice in the mall—Star Simons. What could he possibly have to say to you now?*

M.J.: *Give the boy a chance to explain. Maybe he's come to his senses.*

Plain Jane: *Hello? You're wearing your bathrobe! Your hair is a mess. AND . . . you're not wearing a bra!*

***M.J.:** You're not wearing a bra! Ah, the freedom of it . . .*

Somehow, my fuzzy slippers keep moving down the sidewalk toward the familiar black Jeep Cherokee. My breath comes out in frost clouds. I dig my hands into the pockets of my robe and feel crumpled Kleenex.

Why didn't I pull on clothes? Or brush my teeth? ***Plain Jane***'s right. This is pretty whack. Jackson chose Star over me, and that's that. I have no business coming out here in the middle of the night. I can't even imagine what the rents would do if they saw me. They'd lock me in my room, and through the keyhole Mom would give me the entire birds-and-bees talk all over again.

I slow down as I near the car. The passenger door opens, and Jackson sticks out his head. "Thanks for coming, Mary Jane. You've got to be freezing."

He's right. I am freezing, although I hadn't noticed it before now. I slide into the front seat, tucking my bathrobe under me. It's warm inside, and I see the motor's running. I almost apologize for looking like this, but I catch myself. I'm not the one who should be apologizing. I stare straight ahead, chew on the inside of my cheek, and wait for him to speak.

"Listen," he begins. "Thanks again for coming out in the cold. I just had a craving for a pretzel and—"

I have one hand on the door. ***Plain Jane*** was right all along. He's making fun of me. I am so out of here.

He takes hold of my arm. "Wait! Mary Jane, I'm just kidding. I'm sorry. Please! Let me start over."

Plain Jane is screaming at me to keep going, to step away from the car and not look back.

But ***M.J.*** is whispering about Jackson's forest smell and how good his hand feels clamped around my arm.

I stop struggling, but I refuse to look at him.

Jackson starts over. "I know this is crazy to get you out here in the middle of the night, Mary Jane, but I wouldn't get any sleep if I didn't see you first."

I take a deep breath and turn to him. There's only a sliver of a moon in the sky, but it's enough to throw light across Jackson's face. His brown eyes are intense. I don't think I ever noticed how perfect his ears are.

"I didn't handle that very well in the mall today," he begins.

I don't argue.

"When Star asked me to meet her at Mahoney's, she didn't say you'd be there. I agreed to see her because I wanted to talk to her. Then when I saw you at the table . . . Well, like I said, I didn't handle it very well. And I want to apologize."

"You don't have to apologize to me," I say, not meaning it. "*I'm* not your girlfriend."

No kidding, **Plain Jane** murmurs. *Like his girlfriend would be caught dead in a fuzzy bathrobe and slippers.*

And braless, **M.J.** adds cheerfully.

His hand is still on my arm. It moves up to my shoulder, and I shiver.

"I'm trying to break up with her, Mary Jane. But when I

told her that things weren't working for us anymore, she wigged out on me. I just need a little more time."

I want to believe him. It's not hard to imagine Star wigging out. But I don't want to be wrong.

"Mary Jane, why do you think I kept coming by the Pretzel Twister today?"

"The Twisted Pretzel," I correct. Why he kept coming by there is exactly what I asked myself all day.

"I enjoy being with you, Mary Jane," he says. "We have such a good time when we're together."

Good time? I picture the Mary Jane graffiti on bathroom walls. I shrug his hand off my arm. "Is that what you tell all the guys? Mary Jane is a *good time?*"

He pulls back. "I told you I didn't say—"

"Well, somebody did! My phone's been ringing off the hook. Every guy in Attila thinks Mary Jane Ettermeyer is just waiting to show him a *good time!*"

His lips twitch, and his eyes sparkle. He's laughing, although he's trying not to.

"You think this is funny?" I shout.

The smile vanishes. "I'm sorry, Mary Jane, but we haven't done anything."

"I know that! But nobody else knows it."

He sits back in the seat and asks, "What do you want me to do?" He looks over at me, and I think he's really asking, that he's serious.

"Fix it!" I cry, exasperated.

He drums the steering wheel for a full minute. Then he

says, "I'll just tell everybody it's a lie, that nothing's happened between us."

"You will?" I feel like I've been battling the whole school by myself, and the idea of having someone else on my team makes me want to cry.

"Absolutely," he promises, not taking his gaze off me.

I've come to this car for a fight, but he's making it hard to stay mad at him. "Everybody? You'll tell everybody? How? How can you reach everybody?"

He appears to be thinking this over. Then he says, "Posters?"

The vision of posters proclaiming my innocence in the halls of Attila Ill almost makes me smile, but I keep the smile to myself. "Posters," I say in the same tone my last science teacher used when I said I wanted to fly a kite for my science fair project. "What kind of posters?"

He wrinkles his forehead, and I try not to think about the fact that his face still looks great, even when wrinkled. "I've got it!" he exclaims. "***NOT** Wanted* posters!" He grins, satisfied, as if he's just solved the problem of world hunger. "We'll put your face on the poster and a giant X over it! And below, it will read: MARY JANE ETTERMEYER: NOT WANTED."

I can't help myself. He's making me laugh. I wasn't sure laughter would ever be an option again, but here it is. And it feels pretty good. "It's still not funny," I insist, but I'm saying it with a stupid smile on my face.

He reaches over and touches my cheek. His hand covers the entire left side of my face, making it a thousand degrees hotter than the right side of my face. "I'm really sorry about all of this, Mary Jane. But we'll make it right. We'll fix it together. Okay?"

I can't speak. I don't want to risk jarring his hand from my face.

His fingers move under my hair, to the back of my neck. I can feel each fingertip. "I've never met anyone like you, Mary Jane."

"It's probably the robe," I say, astounded that I can speak, when every neuron in my body is sending wild impulses to all its neuron buddies.

"The robe is undoubtedly part of the attraction," he says, and the moonlight illuminates that dimple.

I can't think straight. My ears are humming. Yet somehow, the voices in my head still manage to come through. So all I can do is repeat what they're saying, more or less:

Plain Jane: *Hello? You're in your bathrobe! You shouldn't be sitting here with him!*

"Look, Jackson," I begin. "I shouldn't be sitting out here with you in my bathrobe."

"With me in your bathrobe?" Jackson repeats. "Don't think it would fit me. Besides, it looks too cute on you."

Plain Jane: *Now you know he's lying! You look like an escapee from a mental institution. Your hair's messed up, and you have no makeup. This fuzzy robe makes you look fat. You are so not cute!*

"Jackson, my hair's a mess. I'm not wearing makeup. And I look like an escapee from a mental institution. The last thing I am is cute."

He scoots closer to me and angles around in the driver's seat so we're right next to each other. "Look at me, Mary Jane. I can't stop thinking about you."

M.J.: *Yeah? And what about the Wicked Witch of the West?*

"Jackson, I don't get it," I manage to say. "You're still Star's boyfriend. Until you break up with her, you and I can't—"

He leans down in the same instant that he tilts my head up. Then he shuts off my words with his soft, full lips and kisses me, long and slow.

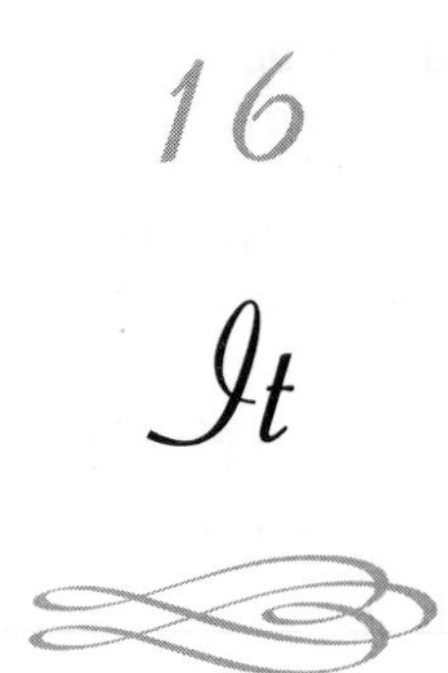

16 It

Sunday morning, Sandy wakes me up by bouncing on my bed.

"Sandy," I groan. It feels like I didn't get any sleep. After THE kiss, I floated back to bed, fully intending to dream sweet dreams. But my eyes wouldn't close, and it's hard to sleep that way. So wide awake, I relived every second I spent with Jackson House. At about 3:00 a.m., I had to get up and chew antacids because it turns out falling in love makes you sick to your stomach. Who knew?

The last time I looked at the clock, it was 4:37 a.m.

"Marwyjan, get ready for church!" Sandy shouts.

I pull the covers over my head.

"What's going on in here?"

From under the covers, I picture Mom in the doorway. She will have her navy suit on and one hand on her hip.

"Mary Jane?" she demands.

I peek out. It's her black suit, but I was right about the pose.

"We're leaving in twenty minutes," she says.

Sandy bounces on the bed as if that will bounce me out.

"I don't feel so great, Mom," I say, and it's true. I feel like you feel when you've been kissed by somebody else's boyfriend and then don't sleep all night until you're bounced by your big sister. Not great. Not even good.

Plus, thanks to the antacids, my mouth now feels like chalk.

Mom's high heels click on my wood floor as she comes over to my bed. "Is this because of that whole boy mess, Mary Jane?" She glances over at Sandy and says, "Honey, why don't you go get your dress on?" Then she lowers her voice. "Your daddy and I are trying to stay out of it and let you handle things."

"And I appreciate that, Mom." I have to hand it to them, actually. I know Dad would love to litigate justice for me, and Mom would like nothing better than to call everybody's mother and make things right.

She gets that funny look on her face and stares at my pillowcase. "Mary Jane, it's been quite a while since you and I had our little talk." She glances at me to see if I get it.

I do. And I'm trying to think how I can get out of listening to the rerun of Mom's version of the secret life of bees and birds.

"You're older now," she begins. "You're probably going to have feelings you haven't had before."

She got that right.

"Just don't do anything you can't undo. Promise that you'll talk to me before—"

"Got it!" I nod appreciatively, signaling an end to this conversation.

Mom cocks her head to the side, as if evaluating whether or not her job here is done.

"Seriously, Mom. Everything's all right," I assure her. "That gossip is being reversed, even as we speak." I picture Jackson dialing guys and setting them straight, fulfilling his promise to help me. "So I'm not hiding out or anything. I just don't feel good."

She leans over and puts her palm on my forehead, the magic mom thermom. "Hmmm. You do feel a little warm. Does your throat hurt?"

"I just need to sleep," I plead. "I'll be okay. You guys go on without me. Sorry."

I actually fall back to sleep until Sandy runs in to show me her church dress before they leave.

Once they're gone and I have the whole, quiet house to myself, I lie in bed and wait for sleep to take over. But the voices in my head are arguing too loud:

Plain Jane: *You don't really believe that Jackson House would choose you over Star, do you?*

M.J.: *Excuse me! We were all in the car last night. He is so into you!*

Plain Jane: *But did you ever ask yourself why Jackson House would waste his time on plain ol' you? Face it. It's not for your bathrobe beauty—I'll tell you that. He's out for one thing. And one thing only. And you can bet he's been getting plenty of that from Star.*

M.J.: *Hey, maybe you're out for the same thing. Did you ever think of that?*

I remind myself that all Jackson and I did was kiss. Once. One great kiss. One super, amazing kiss.

But just a kiss, right? It's not like I've never been kissed before. I *am* a senior. Gary Matthews and I kissed in his car for over an hour last year. I've kissed plenty, even though my membership in AIA (Abstinence in Action) has never seriously been challenged.

Alicia and I used to compare notes all the time. A couple of years ago when she spent the night at my house, we sat on the floor with the lights out in a no-holds-barred, sworn-to-secrecy conversation that lasted the entire night.

"Don't get me wrong," Alicia said. "I'm vowing to stay a virgin until I'm married, in spite of what my mother's instilled in me, not because of it."

Alicia's mother was on her third husband at the time. I didn't think she would have counseled Alicia to lose her virginity, but I wasn't sure. "What did your mother instill?" I asked.

"Oh, the usual," she explained. "Guys won't respect me in the morning, my reputation will be shot, no one will marry a cow that can be milked for free, yadda yadda yadda."

"But you said you agree with her about staying a virgin," I said, pretty confused.

"Yeah," Alicia continued, "but for my own reasons. Sometimes I feel like there's not so much of me to give, so I better save it for the man I want to marry. Like, I don't want to leave pieces of me all over the place. Know what I mean? Plus, who wants to be married to this perfectly great guy but still be thinking about the super sex you had with some loser in high school? It's like tennis."

"Tennis?" It's never been easy following Alicia's thought processes, but the trip is usually worth the trouble.

"Yeah. You know how Meagan and I got to be great tennis partners, but when I teamed with Laura, we stank? I think sex is like that. Like you can learn to be great with one person. So you better be pretty picky and hold out for the right one, the one you're going to be with forever." Then she picked up the nearest pillow and launched into an all-out pillow fight.

Man, I miss Alicia. I know she'll be home for Thanksgiving, but I don't think I can wait. I kick my covers off the bed and climb out. I need to put this thing with Jackson into perspective. I can't let myself get all crazy excited, just to be let down. Been there. Don't want to go again.

When I'm done with my nice, hot bath, I figure Alicia will be awake, so I punch in her number.

"Hello?" Her voice sounds mushy, groggy, like she's half-asleep.

"Alicia? I'm sorry. Are you still in bed? Did I wake you?"

She chuckles. "Yes to the first. No to the second."

I translate. I didn't wake her, but she's still in bed. "Can we talk?"

"Just a minute," she says. I hear shuffling, then footsteps, then a door shutting. More footsteps, water running. Then she's on the line again. "Okay. We can talk now. I'm at the kitchen table."

"You have a kitchen table in your dorm room?" I ask.

"I'm not in my dorm room."

My heart speeds up, and my head doesn't know why. "Where are you?"

There's a second of silence. Then she whispers. "I'm at Colt's. Mary Jane, we did it."

"It?"

"It!"

A million questions swirl in my mind, and the voices are talking at the same time. But I want to hear from Alicia. "Tell me!" I urge.

She sighs, and I picture her face the way it looks when she takes the first bite of chocolate chip cookie dough ice cream. "I don't want to kiss and tell . . . but it was fantastic!"

She sets the scene for me. Candlelight. Pizza. A DO NOT DISTURB sign on Colt's apartment door to keep his roommate away. She takes me right up to *it* and then stops.

I wait for more, but I don't get it. "Wow!" I say at last. I want to be happy for her, but something inside me isn't. I want to ask her if she's totally happy, totally okay with this. I want to ask her about *the pact*.

"I know what you're thinking," Alicia says. "And I haven't changed. I haven't forgotten AIA. It's just that I feel like I've been saving myself for Colt! He's the one, Mary Jane. He's the only one I'll ever do it with. And we'll get better and better together, until we're, like, a hundred years old and can barely do it anymore. But it will be okay because we'll still be so much in love and even like the same TV shows."

I'm busy fighting off the image of Alicia at 100 years old, doing *it*. Then it clicks. "The one? As in he's the one? Alicia? What are you saying? Are you guys talking about marriage?" I can't believe everything's happening this fast. It makes my kiss with Jackson feel like shaking hands with plastic gloves on.

"Not exactly," she admits. "But it's something we both understand. I know he feels the same way, Mary Jane. I can feel it. He wants it as much as I do. We can't stand being apart." She pauses, then says, all breathy, "He said he loves me."

Neither of us says anything, and it goes on too long. Alicia and I have never had phone silence before.

Finally I can't stand it. "Alicia, if you're happy, I'm happy. I guess I just don't know what to say."

"It's okay," she says, sounding like the old Alicia, the one I miss. "We'll talk like crazy when I get home. Hey, why did you call me, anyway?" she asks. "Shouldn't you be in church or something?"

"Jackson and I kissed." I blurt it out, and it sounds stupid now, compared to her news.

But Alicia acts like it's the most exciting news flash she's ever gotten. "That is so tight! You guys are spun!"

"You think?" I ask, her excitement worming its way into me, in spite of myself, in spite of all the barriers I've been trying to build to keep it out. "I guess it *was* pretty terrific."

"That boy is so hot, Mary Jane!"

"He is, isn't he?" I'm coming around now, feeling a little nausea return as I think about his fingers on the back of my neck.

"No lie!" she agrees. "He's the only guy in that whole school I'd ever go out with. If I didn't have Colt, I mean," she adds quickly. "And if he didn't have it bad for my best friend."

"It was just a kiss," I admit. "But it was a pretty great kiss, if I do say so myself."

"And you do," she adds.

"I do indeed," I confirm. "I don't know. It's stupid to make such a fuss over one kiss. It's just that, well, it felt like more. Like the first kiss."

"That is so tight, Mary Jane!" Alicia exclaims. "I know exactly what you mean! When I get back, I want you to tell me every single detail. Promise?"

"I promise. Only there might not be more to tell. He's still going with Star, kind of."

"And she's dating guys behind his back, I'll bet," says my friend the medium.

"Yes!"

"Told you I knew Star. Why does he put up with it?"

"I don't think he knows," I admit. "But he says he's going to talk to her and break up with her. Only you know Star Simons. She's not going to make it easy."

"Nobody said it had to be easy. What are *you* going to do about it?"

"About Jackson?"

"No. About the Queen of England. *Yes,* about Jackson."

"Nothing, I guess. I mean, if he breaks up with her, then I'd love it if he wanted me to go out with him."

"Excuse me," Alicia says. "Didn't you just tell me he was the one in the car with you, the one with the great kiss?"

"Yeah. But if he doesn't go through with breaking up with Star—"

"Mary Jane, it's okay to want Jackson for yourself."

She says it softly, but I hear it as a shout. I *do* want Jackson. "Yeah?"

"Yeah."

Alicia's right. This is an okay thing. On the other hand, this is Jackson House we're talking about. And Star Simons. Barbie and Ken. "Alicia, seriously, do you think Jackson would give up Star . . . for me?"

"Absolutely! Not to mention the fact that he should give up Star for Star. She's trouble no matter how you slice it. And you, Mary Jane Ettermeyer, you are prime time dating material, girl."

We hang up, and I think about everything Alicia said. I, Mary Jane Ettermeyer, am dating material for Jackson House, legitimate competition for Star Simons. I think things are about to get interesting.

17

Aha!

M.J.'s voice rings in my head after I hang up the phone: ***M.J.*** *and Jackson sitting in a tree. I kissed Jackson, and he kissed me!* Sometimes **M.J.** is five.

Grow up! Do you really think you stand a fighting chance against beautiful Star Simons? points out the ever-helpful ***Plain Jane.***

But I'm thinking Alicia is right. Why not admit that I want Jackson House? I want him more than Star does. I would never see another guy if I had the man I love. I don't, and won't, say the love part out loud. I'm sure I don't love Jackson in the same way Alicia loves Colt now. But still. Why should I sit back and cower while Star fights to hold on to Jackson, when the one he really wants to be with is me? You just don't kiss somebody like Jackson kissed me without wanting to be with that somebody. So again, helping Jackson House get what he wants (me), it's kind of a community service thing.

And anyway, haven't I let Star thumb her nose—and give me the finger—long enough? Enough is enough! Jackson and I should be together, and nobody—not even Star Simons—is going to stand in our way.

The rest of the day, I take a stab at homework. But when I'm not thinking about Jackson, I'm thinking about Alicia. And Colt. And Alicia and Colt. I can't wrap my mind around the fact that my best friend has crossed over. She's done *it,* and she's okay with that. I think of a million questions I want to ask her. I try to imagine Alicia married, but I just can't do it.

Red pops into my head. Rianna Elizabeth Douglas. I wonder if Alicia will tell her. Then I have another thought. What if Red and Alex have had sex, too? I could be the only remaining member of Abstinence in Action!

I give up on homework and find Sandy in her room, playing with her plastic horses.

"Will you play with me?" I ask from the doorway.

"I love Marwyjan," Sandy says sweetly, like she's afraid she'll hurt my feelings. "But you aren't too good playing horses. Want to play cards?"

"Deal," I agree.

We move to the family room, and Sandy deals, according to a game Alicia and I long ago dubbed "Go Sandy!" instead

of "Go Fish." Sandy kind of makes up the rules a
along, and the rules are constantly changing.

Changing rules in Sandy's game makes the game n
I'm not sure yet whether the rules I feel changing in
the same effect. I've been waiting all my life for boys t
me. Now I've chosen one. And I'm not sure what the r

We scoot closer to the fireplace and settle cross-l
front of the fire.

"Did boys make you sick?" Sandy asks as she dea
the cards except five.

I'm so stunned by her question that it takes me a
to respond. Sandy and I have never talked about boy
ing or anything related to the topic. I just don't
Sandy like that. "Wh-why are you asking me that, Sa

"Because I heard Mommy. She thought boys m
sick. Did they?"

I have to be careful how I answer. I never wou
imagined that Sandy's thinking would take her here
question. It makes me wonder what else is in her hea
don't know about. Once, when Sandy's kitten di
wouldn't stop crying. All day, she bugged me: "Where'
ley? Where's Smalley?" I tried to make her feel better
stuff like, "Smalley's in heaven with God, Sandy." Sh
and say "Okay." Then an hour later she'd be back w
same question. Finally, I couldn't take it anymore. W
out in the garage, where I was getting my bike to go
where with Alicia. "Where's Smalley?" Sandy asked. Th
it. I pointed up, toward heaven, and said firmly, "Sand

Smalley's up there! He's happier than down here. And that's that." She stopped crying and never mentioned the kitten again, until almost a year later when Dad was climbing to the attic above the garage to get down the Christmas decorations. Sandy came out and saw Dad on the ladder. "Daddy!" she shouted. "Get Smalley!" The poor kid had gone all that time thinking her kitten was in the attic.

I choose my words carefully. "No, kiddo," I finally answer, picking up my cards. "Boys didn't make me sick. They drive me crazy sometimes. But not sick."

"Sometimes boys are nice," she explains. "Sometimes nicer than girls. Chris is."

I remember what Alex said about Chris, Red's brother and Sandy's teammate, and I try to study Sandy's face for signs of embarrassment or confusion or any of the angst I'm feeling about Jackson. But there's nothing.

"Do you like Chris, Sandy?" I ask, almost afraid to tread these waters with her.

She cocks her head to one side and squints at me like I'm whack. "Of course." Then she studies her fistful of cards and demands, "Give me all of your red cards with faces on them."

I give Sandy all of my red jacks, queens, and kings. She places couples down on the carpet in front of her, a jack of hearts with a queen of diamonds, a king and queen of hearts. And a jack of clubs with a ten of spades, just because.

The phone rings, and Mom answers. A second later she hollers, "Mary Jane! Telephone!"

She looks worried, but I know it's Jackson. It's like I can feel him on the phone. We have a connection.

I take the phone from Mom and walk down the hall for privacy. "Hello?" I say in my sexy ***M.J.*** voice.

Mom turns to me with a screwed-up expression. I move farther away.

"Hey, Mary Jane! This is Tim. Wondered if you'd changed your mind about going out with me."

I'm so disappointed that it's not Jackson that I can't even come up with a great putdown for Tim. "Nope. Haven't changed my mind. Won't change my mind." And I hang up.

I tell myself that Jackson just hasn't had time to right all wrongs and restore to me my just reputation. But my stomach's feeling queasy. And when the phone rings again, I'm so startled that I drop my cards.

"Hey, Mary Jane. This is Brad. "So you want to—?"

Before he can finish, I say, "No! Call Jackson!" and hang up.

It takes all the fake confidence I have to convince the rents that all is well and justice will prevail without involving the local police force and the FBI.

I get three more calls Sunday evening, all of them from different guys at school. None of them jocks. Something is definitely fishy. It feels like a fresh second wave of gossip. I explain to each caller that I am not interested, not available, and not that kind of girl.

When the phone rings at 10:00 p.m., I grab it. "What do you want?" There's not an ounce of sex in my voice.

"Uh . . . this is John White? We had algebra together our freshman year until you dropped it."

I can't believe this! John the Math Geek White? "I know who you are," I say, trying to control myself from taking it all out on this . . . this . . . math lover.

"I need to know how far ahead you're booked," he continues.

"Booked?"

"Dated?" he tries again.

"Let me get this straight," I say evenly. "You want to know how far ahead I'm dated up. Are you taking a survey, John? Plan to run the stats and do dating equations?"

"No," he answers, dead serious. "I'd like you to book me for one. One of those dates, I mean."

"What do you mean 'those dates'?" I snap.

"You know. The kind Star said—uh—never mind."

"Star?" Of course! I can't believe I've been so dense! "Star Simons put you up to this!"

"Uh . . . who?"

"What did she say about me, John?" I demand.

"What did who say?" he stammers.

I want to reach through the phone and grab him by his scrawny chicken neck. "Star! I want to know exactly what she said!"

"Aw," he groans. "I don't want to—"

"Now, John!" I scream into the phone.

"She just said you were giving guys a real good time. Things like that. You're not going to tell her I told you, are you?"

"Good-bye, John." I slam the receiver down. Sometimes old-fashioned phones are better than cells that way.

I have to use the phone book to get Star's number. My heart pounds the whole time, not easing a beat as I dial her number and listen to the rings.

"Hello?" I can't believe my luck when Star herself answers the phone.

"Listen to me, and listen good," I begin.

"Who is this?" she asks.

"It's the one you've been spreading rumors about. Although come to think of it, I wouldn't be surprised if you did this to lots of people. So, just so you make no mistake about it, this is Mary Jane Ettermeyer telling you to back off!"

"Mary Jane, are you all right? You sound—"

"Don't even try that two-faced routine with me, Star!" I shout. "I'm so on to you. Just stop it. And you know exactly what I'm talking about."

"Are you finished?" she asks, her voice soft.

I don't answer.

"Just stay out of my business, and I'll happily stay out of yours."

I know she's talking about Jackson.

"You have no idea what my business is, Star. Or Jackson's." And with that, I hang up. The click of the phone never sounded so good.

Before I have time to think, to listen to the voices in my head, I grab my cell and press #1 on my speed dial. I have reprogrammed it to reflect current realities.

Jackson answers his cell on the first ring. "Just Jackson talking," he says.

"Just Mary Jane answering. Jackson, I need to talk."

"I'll be there soon as I can," he promises.

I stare out my bedroom window at the street below, even though I know he can't possibly appear before 10:30 at the earliest. But I wait. And while I wait, the voices in my head come in loud and clear:

Plain Jane: *What are you doing? You know full well that at this very moment, the lines are being drawn. Star is gathering her warriors against you. Your friends are hearing Star's side of this ugly little story of betrayal. You can't seriously believe that Jackson will dump Star for you. So where does that leave you?*

M.J.: *Nothing matters except Jackson. You don't need anyone except Jackson House on your side.*

It's 11:00 before I see Jackson's Cherokee turn onto my street.

I race downstairs, skipping the squeaky step. Mom always leaves the sink light on in the kitchen because Dad's been known to get the late-night munchies. I just hope he doesn't get them tonight.

I ease outside and wish I'd worn a coat instead of counting on my sweater to keep out the night chill. The sky is midnight black and filled with stars that shine brighter than streetlights.

I've rehearsed what I'll say to Jackson. I will calmly inform him that his current girlfriend makes the Wicked Witch of the

West look like Mother Teresa, and the sooner he breaks all ties with her, the better for all mankind. I will further explain that there will be no romance until this whole mess gets straightened out. There will not be one iota of physical expression of affection expressed affectionately between us until my reputation has been restored, and Star Simons is wearing an "ex-girlfriend" tattoo on her forehead. My plan is to remain firm, mature, controlled, yet carefree and fun.

But approximately seven seconds in the car alone with him and every carefully rehearsed line flies out of my head. I stare into his eyes, and I feel my own eyes fill with tears.

He looks alarmed. "Mary Jane? What is it? What's the matter?"

Then I burst into tears. I can't speak. I can't stop crying. All I can do is try to sniff the tears back inside. But it sounds like I'm vacuuming a swimming pool.

"Tell me what's wrong," he coaxes. He puts his arm around my shoulder and pulls me to him.

I don't even feel the stick shift poking into my thigh. All I feel is his hand on my head, smoothing my hair. And I let myself sink into his broad chest. "She's . . . *sniff, sniff* . . . so . . . *sniff* . . . mean!" That's all I can get out.

He hugs me then and rests his head, his chin, on top of my head. "I know. I know. I'll talk to her. I'll make it all okay. Don't worry."

Then before I realize what's happening, he's kissing me. And kissing me.

And I'm kissing him back.

18

The Battle of Attila Ill

I have no idea what to expect when I pull Fred into the senior lot on Monday morning. I don't know if I have any-body left on my side of the battle line. Jackson still needs to talk to Star to tell her they're done, finished, over, history, *and* that she'd better stop spreading lies about me. And I haven't talked to The Girls since the mall.

I'd give just about anything to have Alicia with me right now.

I got up earlier than usual and tried on everything in my closet. It felt like selecting my battle armor.

Plain Jane thought everything made me look fat, but at least my new green sweater was way better than that brown fuzz one that got me into trouble at the mall. She also approved of the tennis shoes, in case I had to flee for my life.

M.J. had her heart set on low-rise jeans, with a low-cut, short red top that would only fly if I got that belly button piercing she's been lobbying for. And if I put on my coat before the rents saw me.

I've ended up with a clothing compromise: tennis shoes, low-rise jeans, green sweater.

Lauren rolls into the spot next to Fred, and we get out at the same time.

"Hey, Lauren," I call as she locks her door and turns toward the building.

She doesn't answer. Her feet move faster.

I'm pretty sure she heard me the first time, but just in case, I holler after her, "Lauren!"

When she keeps going without turning around, I know the battle lines have been drawn, and she's on the other side.

Cassie and Jessica aren't milling around, so I have to walk up the sidewalk alone.

The second I get inside, Jill Sweeny and Emma Phillips charge.

"Listen to me, Mary Jane," Emma shouts. "Stay away from Tyler!"

People are watching, staring. We are the accident they're gawking at.

"Why would I—?" I begin.

"Don't even bother denying it!" Jill snaps. "And while you're at it, keep away from Tim, too."

I didn't know Jill was dating Tim, not that it matters. "I don't know what you've heard, but I haven't done anything."

"Really?" Emma challenges. "Are you telling me you and Tyler haven't talked on his cell?"

"Well, no, yeah, but—"

"Because I have proof! Your number is on his cell, Mary Jane. How do you explain that?" Emma folds her arms as if satisfied that she's caught me red-handed.

"Proof that *he* called *me!*" I can shout, too. "I didn't call him. And I'd be very happy if you had this conversation with him instead of me."

Jill starts to say something, but I cut her off. "And the same goes double for Tim!"

I storm to my locker. But when I glance back, I can see that the opposition is growing. Four girls are circled around Jill and Emma. This is worse than I thought.

I rush to English class because I know Jackson will be there. The room is half empty. I suppose it's also half full, but this feels like a half-empty kind of day. I stop just inside the door and sense eyes turn to me.

Jackson is in the second row, his long legs stretched out and crossed at the ankles. He's laughing with Sean Reed, who plays basketball for Attila, so he doesn't see me yet. It amazes me that Jackson is able to stay on the sidelines of this battle. All evil glares seem to be reserved for me.

I size up the situation and make my decision. Holding my head high, I ease myself into the empty seat next to Jackson. I do this as if it's the most natural thing in the world.

Jackson turns, and his dimple deepens when he smiles at me. "Hey, Mary Jane." He says it like he's very glad to see me. I'm not sure what I expected.

"Hey, Jackson," I return. It will be a miracle if the entire class isn't sweating from the sexual tension between us. Attila High could save on heating bills. Just let Jackson and me sit next to each other in every classroom. I lower my voice. "So? Did you tell Star?"

He winces, kind of like you would if you'd watched your puppy get run over and were just now recalling the scene. "Yeah. She didn't take it very well. She made me promise not to tell anybody we were breaking up until we had a chance to talk things through."

This isn't the report I was hoping for. But at least he talked to her.

Nicole is one seat up and two seats over, and she hasn't quit glaring at me since I walked into the room. "Well, you better finish the job soon, Jackson," I say, "because I'm all alone over here. And everybody's got me labeled as the villain in this thing."

He frowns, looking genuinely surprised. "The villain? How could anybody think that? You couldn't be a villain if you tried, Mary Jane."

I'd like him to repeat this, loud enough for Nicole to hear.

But our teacher interferes and begins class. He writes study questions on the board, and Jackson gets out his notebook and starts copying. The rest of the hour, Schram talks, Jackson writes. Schram writes, Jackson writes.

I try to follow his good example. I do want a boyfriend who takes school seriously. But I'm busy dreading the rest of the long, lonely day ahead.

When English is over, Jackson has to rush off to his next class, and I'm left to shove my way through the Attila High masses by myself. I get so many cold shoulders, I'm numb. The only hopeful sign is that the male population of Attila has stopped pursuing me, apparently. One guy acts suspiciously friendly in French class, but that's it. I give Jackson credit for working his un-gossip campaign behind the scenes, behind enemy lines. Private Jackson, my war hero.

The only one of The Girls who even speaks to me is Cassie. And that's just when I catch her at her locker right before lunch.

"Are you okay?" she asks. She glances nervously over her shoulder, no doubt fearful of having crossed the battle line.

"No, I'm not okay. How would you feel if everybody hated you?"

She risks touching my arm. "Everybody doesn't hate you, Mary Jane. *I* don't hate you."

I'm pitifully grateful for this watered-down declaration of friendship. I tell myself that as soon as Jackson and I are totally together, The Girls will come back to my side. I'll even make a point to include Star, which is something she'd never do for me. I just have to hang on for a while.

I don't even try lunch. Instead, I eat the mints and cough drops I scrounge from my backpack and locker, then hide out in the library with the ax murderer until lunch is over.

The rest of the day slogs by in a nightmarish blur until I happen to run into Jackson after his last class. Could be because I leave study hall early and plant myself in the doorway of his classroom until he exits.

Jackson is in the middle of a group of escaping seniors as he hustles out of the classroom, so I have to shout to get his attention. "Jackson! Over here!"

He glances over at me and smiles his melting smile while I make my way upstream to him. When I get there, I have the distinct feeling that his darting gaze is shooting past me, over my shoulder. Down the hall.

"Could we talk later, Mary Jane?" he whispers. He does that hall-glancing thing again.

I turn to see what he's looking at.

And there's Star. She's walking toward him, smiling. She waves, in her short leather skirt and white cashmere sweater that falls off one shoulder. She's strolling and chatting to Lauren, but she's obviously heading for Jackson.

When I turn back to him, I guess my disappointment is written on my face because he gives me this look that would be an apology if it were words.

"Give me time, Mary Jane. Please?" he whispers. I feel his hand squeeze my arm. Then he moves around me and strides off to meet *her.*

The crowd flows by, jostling me. I am the stone in the river of students eager to leave the building.

I'm still standing there, just outside the classroom, when Nicole walks out. I try to ignore her and turn to go, but I'm not quick enough.

Nicole stops in front of me. "You're making a fool of yourself, Mary Jane," she says. "And if you don't know that, you're the only one in Attila Ill who doesn't."

I was expecting anger in her voice, outrage from the ambassador to the Star. Instead, she sounds sad, sorry. Sorry for *me.* Anger I could handle. But pity?

She comes closer and lowers her voice. "Jackson's playing you," Nicole says. "Star's never going to let him go."

19

Starless Night

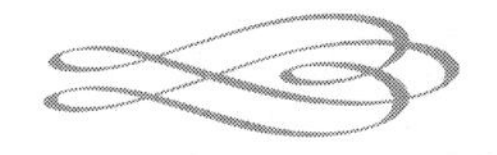

It's all I can do to drive Fred home without swerving into oncoming vehicles. My eyes are tear-blurred. My mind keeps replaying the image of Star and Jackson together, and the voices in my head won't shut up.

Plain Jane: *I knew this would happen. Girls like you always lose in the end. This is why I didn't want you to get your hopes up.*

M.J.: *Hey! Screw him! If he can't see what he's missing, then it's his loss, right? Plenty of fish in the sea.*

My cell rings, and I almost go off the road trying to dig the phone out of my pack. I hate the national anthem.

"What?" I say, slamming on my brakes when I realize the light's turned red.

"Mary Jane?"

It's Jackson. The nerve! Does he think he can talk his way out of this? Keep a little Mary Jane on the side and a healthy serving of Star as the main entrée?

"Go away!" I shout. And I flip the lid on my cell.

A second later it rings again.

I check. It's Jackson. I hit END, hanging up on him.

Again, the national anthem blares. This time I shut off my phone and toss it in the backseat. I will never talk to Jackson House again.

I park Fred in front of the house and run up the sidewalk. All I want to do is get to my room, where I can wail on my bed in private. It's early enough that Mom and Sandy could still be at basketball practice. But when I open the door, I discover that my luck's run out at home, too.

"Mary Jane, I'm glad you're home early!" Mom says, rushing to meet me before I've even shrugged out of my coat. "Your boss at the pretzel shop called. He wants you to call him. He's called twice already."

All I need to make my day complete is a nice talk with the Pretzel Boss. "Can I call him later? I was just going to—"

"You better call him right away," Mom interrupts. "He sounded pretty desperate."

I take the number from Mom and make the call from my bedroom. I try to remember if I told Robbie about my plans to miss THE day. Maybe he let it slip to Pretzel Boss, sending him into a pre-Thanksgiving panic.

Robbie answers the phone. "The Twisted Pretzel. Robert speaking."

"This is Mary Jane, Robbie. I need to speak to the boss."

"Wow! This is the first time you've ever called me. How are you, Mary Jane?"

"The boss, Robbie?"

"Oh. Sure."

A full minute later Pretzel Boss is on the phone, panting. "I need you, Mary Jane!" he shouts.

"I don't work school nights," I inform him. This is only partly true. A couple of times I've gone in after school to fill in for one of the other part-timers. But right now, I'd rather eat my young than twist pretzels.

"You have to come in!" He sounds like he's under attack.

The thought of spending so much as a minute in that den of pretzels makes me even more depressed than I already am, a state I wouldn't have thought possible. "Don't think so," I say.

"Please!" he cries. "It's crazy here! I've never seen it like this."

"Very tempting," I mutter.

"Gina is out sick. Orlando quit. That other boy—what's his name? Ishwan? He broke his arm and just got back from the hospital, and he refuses to come in. You're my last hope!"

"Nice to be first on your list and all, but there's no way I'm working tonight."

"I'll pay you overtime." This is an offer Pretzel Boss has never made anyone.

Even in my whacked-out, beaten-down, exhausted state of depression, I'm starting to realize the opportunity here. This man is desperate. Now that I have no boyfriend, no girlfriends, and nothing at all going on in my life, a career in pretzels seems about right. I should think twice about quitting my job. Plus, how could my day possibly get worse?

"I might come in"—I pause dramatically—"under one condition."

"Name it!"

"Overtime. Plus, I get Thanksgiving Friday off, as in the day after Thanksgiving."

"What? THE day? No way!"

"Nice rhyme," I say calmly. "But my sister has a game I can't miss. So that's the deal. Today or THE day."

Someone's shouting in the background. I think I hear Robbie yell "Help."

"Okay!" Pretzel Boss screams into the phone. "Just get down here now!"

On the drive to the mall, I can't even celebrate this small victory over Pretzel Boss because I'm on my way to Hell's Kitchen, home of the twisted pretzel and the three-cornered hat. Some victory.

When I turn into the mall, I can see why Pretzel Boss was so freaked. I've never seen the Springmill lot this full on a weeknight. I circle the whole complex before taking an illegal spot on the grass.

When I get to The Twisted Pretzel, the line snakes all the way to Nordstrom's.

"Hey! Line forms back there!" barks a four-hundred-pound woman, pointing a stubby finger.

The last place she needs to be is at the front of a pretzel line, but I refrain from telling her so as I slip behind the counter.

"Gloves! Hat! Hurry!" comes the warm greeting of the Pretzel Boss. "You and Robbie both need to wait on customers. I'll cover the oven."

Robbie looks like he's been wrestling alligators. His hat is crooked. Strands of hair hang over his forehead, and he's covered in pretzel dough.

I don't ask.

I get to work, and although I'd never admit it in front of a firing squad, it's good to be this busy with mindless labor. Keeps me from thinking about Jackson. Okay. Keeps me from thinking about him every single second.

Amazingly, I make almost no mistakes in the next hour, and the line dwindles to a dozen or so.

"Your cell's going off again!" Robbie shouts. The mall has piped in Christmas music to drown out the crowd noise, but I've been hearing the intermittent ringing of the national anthem coming from my coat pocket since I arrived. I've chosen to ignore it.

"Let it ring, let it ring, let it ring!" I shout, in tune to the "Let It Snow" music of the moment. If it's Jackson—and it's probably not, because he's undoubtedly moved on to other side dishes—I don't want to talk to him. I have no friends to call me. The only other possibilities would be the football team or maybe the math club. Who needs 'em?

The night wears on, and the screaming, complaining customers help take my mind off Wicked Witches of the West and men like Jackson House, who need a brain, a heart, or a strong dose of courage on their way through Oz.

Finally, Pretzel Boss shouts, "Closing!" I don't think I've ever seen him this happy. He even thanks me for coming in and wishes me a good night.

I'm hanging up my hat and gloves when Robbie comes up behind me.

"Do you want to go out with me tonight?" he asks. But he sounds so tired, I doubt he'd follow through if I said yes.

I don't risk it. "No, Robbie. Thanks for asking."

He shrugs and puts on his orange quilted parka that would come in handy if anybody ever decides to hunt deer in the mall.

I put on my coat and duck under the counter. When I come up on the other side, I'm standing face-to-face with Jackson House.

"Go away," I tell him, even though my heart is pounding holes in my chest.

"I have to talk to you, Mary Jane," he says. He's wearing this long black wool coat that makes him look older and—

"No!" I will not fall for this again. The voices in my head are reminding me how much this guy hurt me, although ***M.J.*** is whispering that he looks so darned good in that coat.

"Please?" he begs. "I've been trying your cell all night. I tried your house, and your mom finally told me where you were."

Robbie comes up behind me. "Everything all right here, Mary Jane?" he asks. I can tell he's trying to make his voice sound deeper. "Is this guy giving you trouble?"

I turn and look down into Robbie's pimply face, screwed into his best tough-guy frown, and I wonder if this is what it feels like to have a little brother. "Thanks, Robbie," I say, with feeling that's real. "I appreciate that. I really do." I turn back to Jackson. "But I can handle this guy all on my own."

I think Robbie makes a relieved sigh. "Well, if you're sure, then." And he walks off, taking time to glare back over his shoulder at Jackson.

I think I love that kid.

"I'm leaving now, Jackson," I say, buttoning my coat. I've put the wrong button in the wrong buttonhole and have to start over. "Better run along. You don't want Star to catch you."

"I deserve that," he says.

"And much more," I agree. "Unfortunately, I just don't have the time." I move past him toward the mall exit. The lights inside the mall dim. The only thing open is the cinema at the other end of the mall.

"Mary Jane!" Jackson calls after me. "Wait!"

I wheel on him then. "Wait? Guess what, Jackson! I'm done waiting!"

Yes! Let him have it! **Plain Jane** cries in my head. *He made you feel like pond scum. And if you're going to get dumped, which of course you already are, you might as well try to take a little dignity with you.*

"What am I anyway?" I shout, stomping back to him. "Somebody you sneak out and kiss when nobody's around to see? Do you have any idea how that makes me feel?"

"It's not like that," Jackson protests. "It was never like that."

"Maybe and maybe not," I say. "But it's not going to be like that anymore!"

Exactly! You tell him! **M.J.** cheers, even though she still thinks he's totally hot in that coat.

"And another thing!" I shout, charging at him, wagging my finger. "The next time I have a date with a guy, he's going to invite me to a movie, right out in the open! Not to his car for a secret kissing session behind his girlfriend's back!" I am on a roll. I am woman. Hear me roar. "What do you have to say to *that,* Mr. Jackson Look-At-Me-I'm-So-Cool House?"

His eyes narrow, and the corners of his lips turn up. He stands up straighter and says, "Mary Jane, will you go to the movies with me?"

"Oh, sure. All you—" I stop. "What did you just say?" My mind is getting fuzzy. The voices in my head are mute.

"I invited you to go see a movie with me," he answers.

"What? When?" I know there are other questions I should be asking. I just can't remember what they are.

"Right here. Right now."

I frown. "Why?"

"Because I am a free man. Because I have officially broken up with one Miss Star Simons. And because I think I just might be falling in love with one Miss Mary Jane Ettermeyer."

"Huh-uh."

He grins. "Uh-huh."

I stare at him and replay what he just said. He's free. He broke up with Star. He's falling in love with me. These are the three best reasons anyone has ever had. For anything. I have no answer.

Cautiously, he puts his arm around my shoulder and starts walking, pulling me with him. "So let's see what's playing."

I'm not sure I've said yes to the movie idea. I'm not sure my legs are moving. But we're gliding toward the other end of the mall, toward Cinema Seven. We're walking together, in step, synchronized.

"It's a school night," I offer lamely, as if anything as ordinary and frivolous as school could have any relevance here.

"I'm aware of that. I'll get you home by ten. Your mother took the time to fill me in on curfews."

My mother? He talked to my mother?

"I don't think she likes guys calling your house," he observes. "So we'll jump in the middle of a movie that gets over in time to get you home. Deal? And it still counts as a movie date. Right?"

He's conversing without me. This is a good thing because I can barely form words in my head, much less let them out for public consumption.

I have to get a grip.

A small line is in front of the ticket booth, and I recognize a couple of guys from Attila.

"Aren't you worried someone will see you?" I ask. "See *us?*"

"Nope. Quite the opposite." He guides me into the ticket line. "Hey, everybody!" he shouts.

People turn around and look at us.

"This is Mary Jane! She's my girlfriend!"

The Attila guys grin and nod. An older couple ahead of us laugh.

Jackson shouts it even louder. "Mary Jane Ettermeyer and Jackson House! Together! No secret here!"

I elbow him because everybody in line, including the ticket takers, stare at us like they're considering a call to mall security. "Okay," I whisper.

"Okay?" he shouts. "Okay! She said okay, everybody!"

Two girls who look like they're in sixth grade and have no business being out on a school night turn around and clap.

The voices in my head are going postal:

M.J.: *Sweet! This is so fly! You are a girlfriend!*

But ***Plain Jane*** refuses to give in to the celebration: *Careful. He's saying this now. But what's Star saying about it? You are so going to get hurt again.*

I shut out ***Plain Jane*** as Jackson buys two tickets to the only movie that ends before ten. Then we walk into the theater hand in hand. Girlfriend and boyfriend.

20

The Girlfriend

I love everybody. As I put on makeup Tuesday morning, concealing the dark circles under my eyes from lack of sleep, I hum Christmas carols.

I am The Girlfriend. The Girlfriend of Jackson House.

Sandy and Mom stop in the hallway outside my room.

"Marwyjan's happy girl!" Sandy announces.

I grin at her and wink. She looks adorable, in purple stretch pants, purple sweater, a purple headband, and thick purple socks.

"Mary Jane," Mom begins suspiciously, "we heard you come in last night."

"I made the curfew." This was only because Jackson made sure I did.

"I know," she says. "I take it that boy found you, then. Jack? Was that his name? Did you make it to a movie?"

I nod. She has entirely too much information. I work very hard to keep my home life and school life separate and unequal.

"How was it? The movie?" she persists.

"Good," I answer, although I didn't see much of it. Mostly we just kissed. Sometime I'd like to be with Jackson someplace where there's no stick shift or armrest.

It feels as if I've been away from Jackson for weeks instead of hours as I pull Fred into the school parking lot. Then I spot Jackson's Jeep Cherokee a few cars over. He gets out and meets me by my car. Jackson House has been waiting for *me.* I can hardly believe this is happening. And it's not even in the middle of the night. *Ta-da!*

Lauren shoots us a few evil glares as Jackson and I walk in together, but I honestly don't care. I want everybody in the whole world to see us together.

We go to his locker. Together. Then we stroll to my locker. Together. Because that's what girlfriends do with their boyfriends.

Tim walks by with Jill Sweeny, and my stomach does its knot-tying trick. But they just smile at us and keep going.

The word is out.

A couple of guys say "Hey" as we thread the halls to English class. Nicole is already in her seat, and I can tell by her fake noninterested expression that she knows.

We take seats next to Sean.

"Hey, man. Mary Jane," Sean says. "Did you hear Brett got new wheels? Some of the guys are going by the garage to check it out after school. You guys can come if you want."

We are already getting couple invites! Finally the grapevine is twisting my way.

"Thanks, man," Jackson answers. "We've kind of got plans. Later, though." He winks over at me.

I didn't know we had plans. But I'm so grateful that I'm not sure I can refrain from jumping on my chair and launching into a cheer.

Schram, just for me, I'm sure, begins a new section in our lit book, the Romantic Poets. He reads a couple of poems out loud, and my face burns because it feels like he's reading to Jackson and me, although Jackson just takes notes like he always does, and I can't tell if other kids in the class are taking in the true, Mary Jane-plus-Jackson meaning of the words.

When Jackson and I have to part and go our separate ways to separate classes, he kisses me. I watch him walk away and feel a lump in my throat. I know it's a cliché, but there it is anyway.

"My locker. Lunch. I want to hear everything." It's Cassie, and she's snuck up behind me and whispered these words. She squeezes my arm, grins, and then hurries off.

I am getting my life back. And then some.

At lunch, Cassie leads me to the cheerleaders' table, and The Girls gather around me. Even Nicole listens as I give them the highlights in the Jackson and Mary Jane Story. Nicole doesn't join in with appropriate girl noises, like Cassie and Jessica and most of the others do, but I can tell she's taking it all in. I think she's still an ambassador.

I finish the story with Jackson waiting for me in the parking lot. Then I turn to Nicole. "Have you talked to Star, Nicole?"

This silences the table, and all eyes are on Nicole now. It's a big moment. She could go for the Star sympathy factor and make things hard on me again. I'm starting to wish I hadn't asked her, at least not in front of The Girls.

Nicole shrugs and takes a sip from her bag of milk. "She's okay."

I'm relieved. Not that I wouldn't ordinarily enjoy seeing Star suffer. But I'm too in love to wish sadness on anybody, even the Wicked Witch of the West.

"I heard she has a date with John this weekend," Cassie offers.

I'm amazed. And then I'm not. I suspected her "love" for Jackson didn't run so deep. If Jackson and I ever broke up—which we won't—I would never have another date for the rest of my life.

I wonder if Jackson knows about Star's date with John. I wonder if he cares. I try not to wonder anymore.

The rest of the school day barely counts because I don't see Jackson. And a world without Jackson? Barely a world. As soon as the bell to freedom rings, I grab my stuff from the locker and hurry to meet my boyfriend.

He told me he'd be waiting for me at the main exit, and

there he is, true to his word. The man is beautiful inside as well as outside. His eyes get bigger when he sees me, and he waves, and I want to feel like this forever.

I keep waving back because I want to be sure that everyone in the halls knows that Jackson House is waving at *me.* Waiting for *me.* His girlfriend.

He turns his head as if he's heard something from the east hall. I look, too.

There, halfway up east hall, coming toward Jackson, is Star Simons. She's smiling and waving at him.

He waves back, though not as enthusiastically as he waved at me.

I hurry down the hall, feeling like I'm in a race with Star.

"Jackson!" she shouts. I hear her over the clamor of the crowd. "I need to talk to you for a minute." She is a train, bearing down the tracks, headed straight for him.

Jackson looks at me. He glances back at her. We are both trains, speeding toward him.

My stomach is churning. I will not go through this again.

I reach him first and stare him straight in the eyes. "Jackson House," I say firmly. "Don't you dare."

He glances at Star, who's just a couple of feet from us now, trying to shove her way through to him, to wedge herself between Jackson and me one more time.

Then Jackson puts his arm around me, and we race out of the building as if it's on fire.

I'm laughing so hard by the time we reach the parking lot

that it's a good thing we're both piling into Jackson's car. I'd never be able to maneuver Fred through the school exit maze.

We snap our seatbelts, and he grins over at me before starting the Jeep.

"Good choice back there, House," I say.

"I thought so," he answers.

We drive around for a while. Then he stops at the DQ for Cokes. He pays. We're a couple.

"So," he begins. "I want to learn all there is to know about Mary Jane Ettermeyer. I know you have a mother. We like to chat on the phone occasionally about curfews and unwanted boy callers."

I laugh and wish I had a tape recording of their conversation. "Was she mean to you?"

"Not after I convinced her I wasn't one of the many boys calling to bug you."

I think about asking him how he managed to convince my mother of anything. But before I can, he has another question for me.

"Who was that who answered the phone?"

The choices are limited. "Deep, male, lawyer-type voice? Man of few words?"

He shakes his head.

"Sandy. My sister." It seems weird that he doesn't know Sandy, like the two people I love the most don't even know each other. "You have to meet Sandy. She's amazing."

"She is, huh? I didn't know you had a sister. Older or younger? Does she go to Attila?"

"She's older but younger, too. Sometimes I think she's like this angel living in our house. She goes to Roy Dale."

"The special school?"

I nod. "And she plays basketball on a Special Olympics team. You *have* to see her play."

"I'd like that," he says. "Can't wait to meet her." He reaches over and tucks a stray strand of my hair behind my ear.

I knew he'd be cool about Sandy. They'll love each other. "By the way," I say, sipping the last drop of my Coke. He's ordered me a regular Coke, and I didn't complain. We haven't been together long enough for him to know I always drink diet. "I like your 'plans' for after school," I tease.

"Do you mind?" He scrunches up his nose, like he actually fears there's anything he could do that would make me mad at him. "I just didn't feel like sharing you with Sean or with anybody else."

This could make me cry if I weren't so completely happy. "Me too," I say. I lean over and give him a kiss. We're still in the car, but it's not the same as our midnight car dates. Nothing is the same.

And I have a feeling—nothing will ever be the same again.

21

Falling . . .

Jackson and I spend every free minute together. We go on walks. We go to the mall, to the grocery store, window shopping. We get lost trying to find a new music store, and we discover we both love detours and getting lost. We even read Keats and Shelley aloud and try to study for our English quiz together. I help him rake the leaves in front of his house. Then I help him jump into them, after we build the biggest leaf pile in Attila, Illinois.

We would spend every minute together if we could. But life interferes. Classes. Sleep. Jobs. Other trivial pursuits. His dad owns a furniture store, and Jackson has to work in the warehouse a few nights a week.

When I'm not *with* Jackson, I'm talking *about* Jackson.

I've used up all my cell minutes on Alicia, and I'll have to move to a land far away when Dad gets our regular phone bill, too.

"I think Jackson and Colt would really like each other," Alicia says one afternoon. It's a rainy Thursday, a week before Thanksgiving, and I'm sprawled on my bedroom rug after detailing the daily Jackson news.

"Sorry. Jackson's spoken for," I answer. But I know they'd get along great, too. "Let's double when you're home over Thanksgiving."

"Deal."

"So," I begin, and this is something I've wanted to ask Alicia all week but couldn't get it out. "Are you and Colt still. . . . still good? I mean, being close and stuff?"

"You mean are we still having sex?" Alicia's always been able to talk about these things more easily than I have. Sometimes I wonder if I ever would have gotten the birds and bees straightened out if it hadn't been for her. Mom's little talk left more questions than answers. "The answer is yes, and it's great," she says.

"Thought so," I reply lamely.

"I went to the health center on campus," she begins.

"Are you okay?" My mind flashes with all the warnings we got from our health teacher in seventh grade when she told us about the dangers of "sex diseases" and STDs and AIDS.

"Yeah. But it's so totally unfair. I mean, guys should have to worry about getting pregnant. Why is it up to us?"

"Good point," I agree, relieved.

"So Mr. Responsible carries a condom in his wallet. Only a twelve percent failure rate. Works eighty-eight percent of the time. Good enough odds for a guy, right? No thank you! So I did it."

"Did what?"

"I marched to the university health clinic in quest of birth control pills. I had to wait two hours in a tiny waiting room, where there was nothing to read except the wall posters of the human reproductive system. Talk about birth control. Those pictures are enough to make you never want to have sex again."

"They always reminded me of Candy Land," I observe. "Or maybe Chutes and Ladders."

"Exactly. Or Operation?" Alicia goes through the painful details of having to confess her "active" sex life to a doctor who didn't really speak English. She finally had to point to the diagram and kiss the back of her hand passionately.

She makes me laugh, but I'm still uncomfortable talking about this. When she finishes, there's a second of silence before I can change the subject.

Alicia jumps on it. "Mary Jane, you're not—"

"No-ohh. 'Course not."

"But you'd like to?"

I don't answer. I've thought about it. I know Jackson has, too. You just don't kiss somebody like he kisses me without at least thinking about it. Besides, he's a guy. They're born thinking about it.

It's turned dark outside my window while we've been

talking. I haven't turned on the lights in my bedroom. I'm glad it's dark.

"Well, take it easy, girlfriend," Alicia advises. "It's a big step. You guys are pretty young. And pretty new as a couple. Don't rush into anything."

"We're not." I don't point out to her that she's only a year older than I am. And I've known Jackson longer than she's known Colt.

"So what are you two doing this weekend?" Alicia asks, probably sensing that I'm ready for a change of topic.

"We're both working tomorrow night."

"Bummer."

"But Robbie's working part of my shift Saturday, so I'm off Saturday night."

"I love that boy," Alicia interrupts.

"Me too. Anyway, Sandy's got a game Saturday night, and Jackson's going with me."

"Sweet! That ought to put him firmly in the Ettermeyer camp. Even if he breaks up with you, he won't want to break up with Sandy."

"Thanks a lot," I say sarcastically. "Everybody loves Sandy best."

"Ain't it the truth."

I actually look forward to going to school on Friday because it's the only time I'll see Jackson. The morning is the best part. Jackson's waiting for me in the senior lot, and we kiss before walking in together. It is so fly to finally be breaking the Attila Ill rules forbidding public displays of affection.

I'm a regular at the cheerleaders' lunch table, and I talk so much that I barely get my taco eaten before it's time to bounce to class. But I've skipped breakfast, so I'm hungry enough to stay behind and stuff down the remaining tortilla.

Only Nicole is still at the table when I gulp the last bite. I get the feeling she wants to say something to me.

I break the ice. "So are we okay, Nicole?"

She lets out a sigh, like she's relieved to have me ask. "I am if you are, Mary Jane. I hope you're not mad about things. I mean, before. I've just . . . you know. Star and I have been friends for a long time. I didn't want her to get hurt."

"Is she?" I ask. The cafeteria is emptying, but I figure this might be worth getting to class late.

"She's okay."

"Is she really going out with John?" I ask. It's more than a casual interest. I would like to see John and Star get married, have a dozen kids, and move to California. This week.

She shrugs. "I guess." She leans closer. "But she's waiting."

"Waiting?" The taco has stopped its trip down my digestive tract. "Waiting for what?" But I think I know this answer. I think I knew it all along.

"For Jackson. She says you have him for now, but you won't do what it takes to keep him."

I study Nicole's face for signs that she's saying this to get to me, that it's a secret mission in her role as ambassador. But there are no such signs.

I'm not twelve. I know what Nicole's talking about. Jackson's not twelve either. Plus, he's a guy. A guy who was getting what he wanted from his last girlfriend.

Nicole gets up from the table. "I just thought you ought to know, Mary Jane. And I'm glad you and I are okay."

She may be okay. I, on the other hand, feel like someone's just burst my balloon, wrecked my car, run over my puppy.

I stay in the cafeteria until the cafeteria ladies and I are the only ones left.

I feel like walking straight to Fred and punting the rest of classes, but I don't. Instead, I get yelled at for being late to class. But I don't care. My mind is spinning, and the voices in my head are at it again:

Plain Jane: *I'm so not surprised. You're in the big leagues now. Maybe knock-out gorgeous women can keep a boyfriend without sleeping with him, or at least giving him some kind of sex, but not ordinary girls with zits on their chins. You were not destined to be a girlfriend.*

M.J.: *Hey! Girls like sex, too. It's not just a guy thing.*

I try to shut out the voices because they're making me more confused than I already am. I know I was just a kid when Alicia, Red, and I made our pact to wait until we were married. But the reasons were good, and they haven't changed, even if I have. If all that was true then, isn't it true now?

Alicia's already grown out of the pact, and I wonder if Red has, too. I want to ask her. I don't want to be the only member of Abstinence in Action, especially if it really means losing Jackson.

But this is whack. Jackson hasn't asked. We're still enjoying getting to know each other. And kissing and being close.

I wish I'd never talked to Nicole.

The rest of the day, I do my best to put the whole thing out of my mind and go back to being happy with my boyfriend. And by the time school's over, I'm almost back to inflated balloon, shiny car, and healthy puppy.

I hate it that Jackson has to leave right after school. We walk to the senior lot together and find Fred. I lean against the driver's door, and Jackson kisses me. "At least we'll both be miserable in the land of the employed tonight," he offers.

"No chance we could see each other before my pretzel shift starts?" I touch his ear because it's so perfect and because I can.

He shakes his head. "I'm late already. And Dad's got me closing the store tonight. You could come by after you're liberated from the Pretzel Boss, though."

Yes! "Okay."

We kiss once more, and I start counting the minutes until I'll see him again.

I can't stop smiling during my tour of duty at The Twisted Pretzel, even when a crazed, multi-pierced biker-shopper calls me an idiot because I salted his frosted cinnamon pretzel. Not even when Pretzel Boss threatens to back out on our deal and make me work next Friday. And not even when Robbie asks me to go to his senior prom with him . . . in three years.

Jackson calls my cell six times, at regular intervals, and tells me that he misses me. I love the national anthem.

Robbie agrees to close, so I skate as soon as the clock strikes nine. Fred and I cross town back to Main Street, Attila, Illinois, where Jackson's dad has his furniture store, as did his dad before him and *his* dad before him. The House of Furniture, which I'm thinking is some kind of House family–furniture store play on words, stands tall between Picture This, our only professional photography studio, and Wilson's Drugs, a pharmacy that sells everything from coloring books to ironing boards.

I park Fred out front and walk to the door. It's pretty dark inside, except for one light coming from the back. The sign is flipped to CLOSED. I knock on the glass. The night air is chilly, and it smells like snow's coming. I glance across the street at the giant candy canes dangling from the streetlights. The whole town decorates itself for Christmas before Thanksgiving even has a chance. Someday I'll run for mayor and change all that. But tonight I even like the candy canes.

The door opens, and I spin around.

"Come on in," Jackson says, holding the door open for me.

I scurry inside, and he shuts the door behind me. Then he walks over and wraps his arms around me. We hug for a full minute before we kiss.

They could make a movie of us.

"C'mon. I'll show you around." He takes my hand and jogs toward the single light hanging above an old wooden door. He pulls the door open, and I peer behind it. "That's the warehouse, where I've spent more hours than child labor laws allow."

"You poor boy," I say, squinting into the darkness. I can make out boxes against the nearest wall and maybe some recliners farther back.

"Enough of that," he says, racing to the far side of the showroom and pulling me with him. He stops in the dining room display and sweeps his arm at the surrounding furniture as if he's a boat-show girl showing off the latest yachts. "We have here a solid oak country table, with two panels available and matching solid wood chairs."

"I'll take them," I say. "And I want that couch." I point to the front of the store, where a perfectly ugly white couch sits, covered in plastic. "Because I feel sorry for it. This is the way I buy our pets, too. And boyfriends. I always end up getting the ugliest of the litter, the ones I'm positive no sane person would ever go home with."

"What?" He lets go of my hand and acts totally offended. "Are you making fun of my couch?"

"More like mocking, really," I explain. "And not just the couch. I better take that poor chair over there, the one with wagon wheels. Oh, and that hideous clock over there, and—"

"That's it!" he shouts. His eyes narrow, and his voice gets gravelly and villainous. "Nobody, and I mean nobody—"

"Which is why you said 'nobody'?"

"*Nobody* mocks the House of Furniture and lives!" He creeps toward me, a step at a time, clawlike hands raised dramatically. "You will pay for this, wench!"

I dart around the table just as he reaches for me. "Nobody said I had to *pay* for this junk!" I cry.

He laughs evilly and stalks toward me. I run behind a leather couch and crouch down, but he leaps over the back of the couch and lands inches from me.

I scream and laugh as I weave around chairs. He chases me. I scramble under a table and come dangerously close to knocking over a lamp. I'm in the darkest corner of the store, where I keep bumping into things. It doesn't help that I'm laughing so hard I can barely catch my breath.

I can tell I'm in the bedroom showcase because I just banged into two dressers. I make a dash for the bed and plan to hide under it, but there's a fake bottom, like in hotel rooms, so you don't leave your socks under the bed.

"Gotcha!" Jackson grabs me around the knees, and we tumble onto the mattress together. I squirm, but he's got me. "Laugh at my furniture, will you?" he says in a horrible Eastern European accent. "Theeze eeze what I do to people who mock zee House of Furniture!"

He tickles me, and I explode into fits of laughter. He's ruthless and unrelenting.

"Stop! I give!" I cry. "House of Furniture rocks! I love that couch! You win!"

He stops and leans back to sit on his heels. "That's more like it."

I'm spent from running and laughing. And only in this second do I realize that I'm alone with Jackson. On a bed in his father's store.

22

And Falling . . .

The second I realize where I am, in bed with Jackson House, I think Jackson realizes it, too. He stops talking. He stops laughing. The single bulb hanging from the ceiling makes his face a black silhouette above me as he leans down and kisses me.

I kiss him back. He relaxes into me, against me. And then he gently rolls on top of me. I can feel myself soften under him, into him, until I'm not sure where I leave off and Jackson begins. I've never felt like this before. It's happening too fast, like I'm in an ocean, pulled by the tide. And we're rocking in waves together. I can't think. I hear the voices in my head telling me I'd *better* think, and think fast.

"Wait," I say.

He stops kissing me.

"I'm sorry," I whisper.

He leans back. "Mary Jane, I love you. You know that, right?"

"I love you, too." If I'd had any doubts about it before, I don't now. "But this is . . . I mean, I'm not . . . Jackson, I don't want . . ."

He pulls away from me and sits on the edge of the bed, his head in his hands. "It's okay, Mary Jane."

"Promise?" I ask. It doesn't feel okay. I don't want to think about Nicole's warning, but now her voice is in my head. Like I need another voice there.

He turns and smiles at me. "Promise. And just so you know, I didn't plan this, in case that's what you're thinking."

I hadn't been thinking that, but it's nice to know just the same. "I know. I'm the one who mocked your couch and started this whole business."

"That's true," he agrees. He stands up, and I climb off the bed. He reaches behind me and straightens the bedspread. "What do you say we blow this firetrap?"

As soon as I get home, I dial Alicia. When she doesn't answer her cell, I try her dorm. But she doesn't answer there either. What good is a best friend who isn't even there when you need her?

I consider calling Nicole, but I know better. She'd go straight to Star. Cassie has a date, so I can't call her. I'm not sure this is something I can talk about with The Girls anyway.

There's a knock at my door, and Mom sticks her head in.

She's wearing a light blue flannel nightie that looks very mom-ish and somehow makes me feel better. "Everything all right?"

"Yeah. Why?" These words are out before I think about them. They are my automatic responses to most questions posed by my rents. I think about taking them back, though, because I'm not entirely sure that everything is all right.

She smiles and tiptoes into my room as if I'm still asleep, and she might wake me. "You were making funny noises in here. Groans. Grunts."

I make a mental note that I'm too young to start making such sounds. "I was trying to get hold of Alicia."

She tiptoes a few more steps and sits on the corner of my bed. "It's pretty late. Must have been important."

You can talk to your mom! ***Plain Jane*** says.

Get real! **M.J.** counters. *Your mother probably hasn't had sex since you were born.*

"You seem to be spending a lot of time with this Jackson guy." Mom smoothes out nonexistent wrinkles in my bed-spread. "You must like him a lot."

"He's pretty likable," I agree, not sure where we're going with this. Not sure where I want to go. She's met Jackson a few times when he's come by for me. Dad's even met him once. Sandy sleeps so much that she's missed him every time he's come by. But Jackson will get to meet Sandy at her game.

Mom smiles at me. She's not wearing any makeup, and it

strikes me that she looks good this way. Or maybe it's just the bad lighting in here. "I want you to know that if there's anything you want to know . . . about boys, men . . . well, you can ask me anything."

"I know." I probably do believe this. I just can't quite imagine myself taking her up on the offer.

"And sex." She goes back to smoothing bedspread wrinkles. "You know how your father and I feel about sex."

"Okay. Promise you won't put yourself, my father, and sex in the same sentence ever again."

We both laugh nervously. But I know she's trying hard to be a mother here. So I try to help. "I know. Like, don't do it, right?" This is exactly what I would tell my daughters if I were the mother.

She smiles at me and doesn't look away. "I probably would have put it differently, like how beautiful the act of love is when there's commitment and safety and love and marriage. But it would have boiled down to the same thing, I guess." She stands up, then leans down and kisses my forehead. "Night, Mary Jane."

I take a long bubble bath and fall back into bed. And when I finally drift off to sleep, I'm too tired to dream and too tired to listen to the voices in my head.

Jackson calls me as I'm driving Fred to the mall for Twisted Pretzel duty Saturday morning. I'm relieved when he acts as if nothing weird happened last night.

"I better meet you at Roy Dale," he says after we've talked lovey-dovey mushy for a few minutes. "Dad's doing inventory. I can only get away a couple of hours. I'll be there before the game starts, but I'll have to leave early. Dad says we'll be at it all night. And get this. He loves inventory."

"Was your dad genetically engineered from the same lab as Pretzel Boss? Just asking."

"Yep. They were running a sale on them that year."

"You're going to love Sandy, you know," I tell him before he hangs up.

"No doubt. I'm a softie when it comes to Ettermeyer women. That and those round chocolate mints with the candy coating. You know, like they give you after dinner at fancy restaurants?"

"You sweet talker. See you later."

I'm almost late to Sandy's game because Pretzel Boss mutated into Pretzel Nazi and threw a fit that I'd dare break ranks before my shift ended, even though Robbie was already there to take over.

I run inside Roy Dale and hear balls bouncing and crowd noise coming from the gym. I'm relieved to see Sandy out on the floor with her whole team, still warming up. She's holding a ball and looking all around until her gaze stops on me. Then she drops the ball and lumbers up to me.

"Hi, kiddo!" I shout, meeting her halfway on the sidelines.

She lunges at me and throws her arms around my neck. "Marwyjan!"

I squeeze her back. That's when I see Jackson waving at me from the bleachers. "Sandy, there's somebody I want you to meet."

She releases me. "Okay."

I take her hand and lead her over to Jackson, who's already on the sidelines walking toward us. "It's a boy," I whisper.

"Okay."

We meet Jackson on what would be the fifty-yard line if we were on a football field instead of a basketball court. He's wearing jeans and a black sweater, and I hope everybody in the gym can tell he's mine all mine. "Sandy," I say, nodding to Jackson, "this is Jackson House. Jackson, I'd like you to meet my sister, the Dragon, Sandy Ettermeyer."

Jackson reaches out and shakes hands with Sandy. "I've been wanting to meet you for quite a while. I'm really looking forward to seeing you play, Sandy. I've heard a lot about you and the Dragons."

Sandy gives him her cutest smile, which is so darn cute I can hardly stand it. "Purple," she says, holding her shorts out like she's going to curtsy.

"I love that color," Jackson claims.

Sandy grins again, then turns to me. "Does *this* boy make you sick, Marwyjan?"

"Not so much," I answer.

To his credit, Jackson doesn't so much as guffaw.

From the bleachers comes a piercing whistle that could only originate from Red. I spot her behind the Dragon benches, sitting next to Alex. She waves us over. Jackson and

I have already talked about Red and Alex. He remembers Alex from school. We make our way over to them, and I do the introductions.

Red says "Hi" to Jackson, then hops off the bleachers to give Sandy a big hug. "I've missed you, sugar!"

"I missed you, too." Sandy touches Red's purple jogging suit. "You like purple! I like purple!"

"Yep," Red agrees. "Purple rules!"

"I've missed you, too, Red," I say, grinning at her. She looks great. Her hair is longer than I remembered. I think she's put on a couple of pounds, but they're in the right places.

"Good to see you, Mary Jane," Red says. She turns back to Sandy. "You know, Sandy, Chris says you've gotten to be a really good player."

"Uh-huh," Sandy agrees.

I love this about my sister. There's not an ounce of conceit in her answer. She just happens to agree with Chris and doesn't pretend anything else.

The buzzer sounds, and Sandy joins her team.

Jackson and I scoot in next to Alex. Red is already on her feet, yelling, "Go, Dragons!"

"You Ettermeyer women just keep getting better and better," Jackson says. "Now I see why you talk about Sandy the way you do. She's really something. I can tell that, and I've only known her two minutes."

I lock arms with him and lean in as close as I can. I don't think I've ever felt more in love with Jackson House.

Chris scores from the opening jump, and Red goes crazy. Alex knows exactly what to say to calm her down. There's something in the way he says "Red." It calms me down, too. Red and Alex could rent themselves out as the Zoloft alternatives. Just being around them makes me less anxious. With some couples, I always feel in the way, no matter how nice they are. I can't shake the feeling that they're just waiting until they're alone again. But Red and Alex make everybody feel like family.

It's a great first half, with lots of up-and-down action, and the four of us spend more time on our feet than we do keeping the bleachers warm.

At halftime, we lead 22 to 14. Jackson and I make an appearance and chat up my rents because I can't see my way out of it. He talks to Mom as if they've known each other for ages, and she doesn't stop talking, even when I try to make our getaway. She keeps filling him in on the whole Dragon team. Dad says "Hello" when we walk up to their bleacher and "Nice to see you again" when we leave.

Jackson has to take off at the start of fourth quarter. He gives me a kiss, right in front of the Dragons, the rents, and everybody, and hollers good-bye to Sandy, who leaves the bench and runs over to give him a hug.

"He's nice," Red says after he's gone.

"*I* think so," I agree. "He's my boyfriend," I add, grinning like when we were ten.

"I noticed."

I don't think I realized how much I've missed Red. I always thought of her as more Alicia's friend than mine because they were in the same class. But Red couldn't have been cooler to me in high school. And if I really needed help, I always knew I could count on her.

She trades places with Alex so she and I can sit next to each other. I watch the way Alex watches her as she moves past him on the bleachers. His hands are raised slightly, ready to catch her if she trips. He touches her arm as she sits down. If there really is a look of love, that boy has it for Red.

"So how long have you and Jackson been going out?" Red asks.

I give her the highlights in between bursts of cheers for both teams. Sandy gets fouled and has to shoot two shots from the "mistake line." She misses them both. But when the second one hits the rim, her team cheers for her. Chris rushes over and gives her a hug, then gets a rebound and scores.

"Chris is crazy about Sandy, you know," Red confides.

"Yeah?" I glance at Alex, and the way he grins tells me he already knows this bit of information.

"Tell her about the phone call," Alex urges.

Red sits down. "Okay. So Alex and I are making popcorn. But we hear Chris talking back in Dad's den. And we don't mean to eavesdrop—"

"Yeah, right," Alex interrupts.

She punches his arm. "So we hear him talking about basketball and figure out he's called Sandy."

"Since he'd asked Red to write down Sandy's number for him that morning," Alex chimes in.

"I never knew he called her." I wonder if Mom knew, if Sandy told her, why Sandy didn't tell me.

"You might have been on pretzel patrol," Red suggests. "Anyway, we hear Chris ask Sandy if he could kiss her."

"No way!" I can't stand that this happened and I didn't know anything about it.

"Yep," Red continues. "He even said 'please.'"

"What did Sandy say?"

"We couldn't hear her part of the conversation," Alex explains. "But we figured our boy got shut down in a nice way."

Red picks it up from there. "Because there's a little silence. And then, without missing a beat, Chris asks her if she likes Bugs Bunny or Spider-Man best."

That makes me laugh. It's the kind of nontransition Sandy would make, too.

"Chris didn't even seem upset or let down or anything," Alex continues.

"Still," Red muses, "I wish I had a recording of that call. I sure would like to know what Sandy said."

The rest of the game, I keep one eye on Sandy and Chris and the other on Alex and Red. Sandy doesn't treat Chris any differently from the other players. I think I catch Chris staring at Sandy a couple of times, but neither of them appears nervous when they're standing close together. I make a mental note to ask my sister about Chris's phone call when we get home.

Watching Alex and Red tells another story. They hold hands and laugh at shared jokes. The voices in my head do a running commentary on the couple:

Plain Jane: *Now there's a real couple. And an extremely handsome couple at that. Look up* cute *in the dictionary, and you ought to find a picture of Alex and Red. They're the real deal.*

M.J.: *Look how they can't keep their hands off each other. They're either holding hands or linking arms or playing footsie. They are so doing it!*

I try to put the thought out of my head. But the whole world has turned into couples for me. And as I gaze around at the couples seated in the gym, the one question on my mind is whether or not these couples are doing *it*.

I want to talk to Red, but I can't. Not with Alex around. She's only home on weekends. I can't ask her to give me time that she could be spending with Alex.

But I need to talk. I still haven't been able to get Alicia on the phone. And anyway, Red's the one I want to talk to now. I want her to tell me how Alex and she can stay in love for so many years.

With less than a minute to play, I break down and ask, "Red? Do you think Alex could spare you for an hour after the game? I hate to ask. But I need to talk."

She smiles at me, then turns and says something to Alex.

He grins over at me. "Not a problem."

The buzzer sounds, and it's another victory for the Dragons.

We congratulate Sandy and Chris and the players on both sides. Then Alex, Red, and I make our way to the parking lot. Alex walks with us to Fred.

"Thanks, Alex. I appreciate you loaning me Red. I'll get her back ASAP. Promise."

"Hey, the good Lord wants us to share, right?" He frowns at Fred. "Just bring her back in one piece?" He kisses Red quickly, but she keeps hold of his hand and pulls him back. Then they exchange a real kiss.

M.J. is screaming in my head, *They are totally doing it!*

When they're done, Alex looks like a little boy who's just been caught stealing cookies.

"So you guys are still in love, huh?" I observe.

Red turns to me, hands on hips. "We hold these truths to be self-evident!"

"What she said," Alex agrees.

I laugh hard, because history-loving Red has always used this line from the Declaration of Independence instead of "Duh," like the rest of us.

Red and I drive around for a while and talk about everything except what's really on my mind. Then I pull in at a fast food, and we get fries to share.

"Alicia's coming to the next game the day after Thanksgiving," I tell her.

"Man, I'd like to see her!" Red exclaims. "I'm so bummed

that I have to miss the game. Now I'll miss Alicia, too. We kind of lost touch."

"Why can't you be here?"

"Alex and I are going to California for Thanksgiving break. It's time to visit Alex's dad and the new wife."

"Is he close to his dad?" I kind of remember when his parents got a divorce. I don't think Alex saw his dad much after that.

"Nope. Not sure about this new wife either. She's just a couple years older than we are. She thought Alex was kidding when he told her we needed separate bedrooms."

I know I'm not going to get a better opening than this. "Separate bedrooms, huh? Guess that means you're hanging on to your membership in AIA." I make it a joke, but I wait for an answer.

Red shakes her head, then turns to me. "Abstinence in Action. Man, was that like a thousand years ago? I haven't thought about that for a long time."

I knew it!

"We were pretty smart for kids, huh?"

"We were? I guess."

She narrows her brown eyes and lets me know she's on to me. "Okay. I may not have thought about our pact for a while, but I sure do think about abstinence all the time. I have to." She laughs. It's the same laugh I remember—loud, unrestrained, out there. "I have to because being around that man of mine can't help but make me think about sex." She sighs deeply. "He is *so* sexy, isn't he?"

"But . . . but you mean . . . you and Alex haven't . . . you're not—"

"Nope."

"But you're so much in love."

"Which is *why* we're waiting until we get married."

"Isn't it hard?" I think of Jackson and me on that bed in his furniture shop, and I shiver inside.

"We hold these truths to be self-evident." Red turns in her seat and draws her knees up, so she's sitting on her feet, just like she used to do on my bedroom floor when she and Alicia came over to listen to music. "Okay," she begins, "sex is intense. Even if you're positive you're not risking AIDS or STDs, sex changes everything in a relationship. It takes over and grows without any effort at all. Communication takes effort, so why work at that anymore? Then you've got this intense, confusing relationship with nowhere to go."

I wish Alicia were here to make her case for true love and true sex. I'd much rather sit in the background and listen to the two of them debate. "What about Alex? How's he handling it?"

"Alex and I have our own pact. He's coming from a different place. You know how much that boy believes in God."

I'm uncomfortable now, so I try to lighten us up. "So he's afraid God will zap you if you have sex?" I laugh, and so does she.

"No way! Alex says sex is God's thing. God made the equipment, and he knows when it ought to be used to get the most out of it. And we plan to get *the most* out of it, girl. You just wait for the earthquake that's going to register on that Richter scale on our wedding night!"

We're quiet for a minute. I can't bring myself to ask her all the other questions the voices are shouting in my head: *How does she stand it? Isn't she afraid she'll lose him? Does she feel like they're the only ones waiting?*

I steer the conversation back to Dragon basketball until I drive her home.

"Thanks for the fries, Mary Jane," Red says when I pull up in her driveway. "Tell Alicia to call me or e-mail." She gets out of Fred but leans in before she shuts the door.

"I'll tell her," I promise. "And thanks, Red. I know you think I'm crazy. But I needed tonight. Things have been getting kind of confusing lately."

She grins and winks. "Mary Jane, we hold these truths to be self-evident."

23

The Plan

All week I count down minutes to Thanksgiving break. Then the last day of school, Jackson shows up with bad news. As in Paul-Bunyan-sized bad news.

"My mom was on the phone half the night with my grandmother. Gram's got a cold. They can't come down here for Thanksgiving, so we have to go up there. We're leaving today, Mary Jane."

"No!" I protest. "Can't you stay home without them? You could have Thanksgiving dinner with us." As soon as I say it, I know it's a bad idea. Thanksgiving at the Ettermeyers' has the potential to destroy relationships. My uncle used to bring a different date every year, but it usually ended up being his last date with said girlfriend-of-the-year. He and my dad have an unspoken rivalry that sometimes gets spoken on Thanksgiving.

Jackson is shaking his head. "I tried everything, including claiming that I've developed an allergy to turkey and sweet potatoes. No way out. We're driving to Oak Lawn right after I get out of class."

"Today?" It's starting to sink in. "You're leaving today?" That means I won't see him tonight. Or tomorrow. I don't know if I can stand being away from him that long.

His arm tightens around me. "I know. Believe me, I'd stay home if I could. But listen. It could work out for us, Mary Jane."

I can't imagine how his being gone could possibly work out for us.

"I talked them into driving two cars. Dad got a deal on some lamps and end tables my grandma's been looking for. He's filled the backseat of his car. So he was glad to have me drive and take the rest of the boxes."

"Still waiting to see how this works for *us*," I say impatiently.

"I'm getting to that part." He puts his hands on my shoulders and leans down so his face is an inch from mine. "They're going to stay the whole weekend, and I'm driving back alone on Friday."

It's not as good as if he were staying home the whole time, but it's better than nothing. I lean my forehead against his. "Good. Because there's no way I could wait until Sunday to see you again."

"Mary Jane, it's not just good. It's perfect!" He wraps me in his arms. "We can finally get some time alone. We need this, babe. We'll have the whole house to ourselves." He strokes my hair, and hot chills race through my body. "I want this to be so special, Mary Jane." He leans down and kisses me. "This is going to be *our* Thanksgiving. Friday's *our* night."

We're almost late going inside, so we split to our own lockers. As I watch him walk away, the voices in my head are screaming:

Plain Jane starts out sounding strangely like my mother: *Do you realize what that boy has in mind? What he's planning? Use your brain, girl! Just say no! What about the vow? And the cow who will never be married because it gives its milk for free?* Then she segues into her normal, insecure voice: *This is what he wanted all along. I guess if you want to keep him, you have to go there. He's used to Star, who no doubt has plenty of experience in this area. You're going to disappoint.*

M.J., on the other hand, is busily running through a growing to-do list: *You have forty-eight hours to get your hair done, nails done, shave, shop. I've always told you underwear should be purchased at Victoria's Secret, not Wal-Mart.*

Part of me is complaining that everything is moving too fast. But the other part of me, the part that feels like I've known Jackson forever, is cheering that it's about time.

But am I ready? Ready for *it?* Things were so simple back when the founding fathers—mothers—formed Abstinence in

Action. I think I still believe the things we said when we made our pact. And Red made perfect sense. I know I only get one "first." I know it would be the best thing if it came on my wedding night, rose petals strewn on the honeymoon bed—this is how I've pictured it.

On the other hand, Alicia's broken the pact, and her world hasn't fallen apart. Maybe Jackson isn't even thinking of *that*, exactly. Maybe he's just thinking of the imagined "missing-four-minute" version of *that*. But that's close enough.

We have early release for Thanksgiving, giving us another reason for thanks. Jackson and I stroll to the senior lot, our arms around each other. "Couldn't we just run away to Plymouth Rock or something?" I suggest.

His arm tightens around my waist. "Just keep thinking about Friday." He sounds happy and excited. "Just tell me you're okay with Friday night."

I look up at him. He is so amazing. How could I *not* be okay? "Are you kidding?"

He lifts me off the ground and spins me around before setting me down slowly. "I love you, Mary Jane."

"Me too you."

We hold hands as we walk to Fred.

"Any chance you'll get back in time for Sandy's game Friday?" I ask. "Sandy would love it. And Alicia's going to be there with her boyfriend."

"I'll try, okay? I'd love to watch Sandy play again. And I

don't think I've seen your friend Alicia since she graduated. No guarantees, though. I'll call your cell when I'm on the way back, okay?"

We're standing beside Fred, and I know it's time to go. "Well . . . " I say, but I'm fresh out of words. I know it's only two days, but I can't imagine forty-eight hours without him.

Jackson reaches out and touches my cheek. "You're beautiful, Mary Jane Ettermeyer. You know that? And I can't wait to have you all to myself. Don't worry about anything. I'll take care of everything. I'll take care of you."

I'm not sure I've ever felt this beautiful. Even ***Plain Jane*** in my head isn't arguing the point.

Jackson leans down and kisses me, so deep and so full that every other thought dissolves. "Until Friday," he says when we come up for air.

My legs feel wobbly, but I manage to get into my car. I smile through the window at Jackson, amazed that someone like Jackson House would choose me. "Until Friday," I promise.

24

Thanksgiving

When Fred and I pull into the drive, I half expect to see Alicia's VW there, just like old times. But the driveway is empty. I've only talked to Alicia once all week, and she was in a hurry for class, but I know her break starts today. I've calculated how long it should take her to drive home from the university, and she should be here by now, unless traffic was worse than I thought. I'm bursting to tell her everything. If she doesn't get here soon, I'll make her spend the night, and we'll have a no-holds-barred, tell-all marathon. Colt will have to fend for himself.

I jog inside. Mom and Sandy are on the couch, watching something that features annoying, squeaky cartoon voices.

"Hi, guys! Did Alicia call?"

"No." Mom looks up from the giant recipe file on her lap. "Do you think you remember Aunt Jill's recipe for that cranberry-marshmallow salad your dad loves? Because I can't find it anywhere."

"No." I hang my coat on the one empty hook by the door. "Are you sure Alicia hasn't called? No messages?"

"No. Oh, and don't forget," Mom reminds me. "You need to make your overnight salad for dinner tomorrow."

"I will," I promise. "I'm going up and call Alicia."

I shut the door to my bedroom and dial Alicia's house. I haven't dialed it since she left for college, but the number's tattooed in my brain.

A man answers. Probably Alicia's current stepfather. "Yeah?"

"This is Mary Jane. Is Alicia home?"

"Just a minute."

Several minutes later Alicia's mother picks up. "Hello?"

"Hello . . . " I have momentary brain freeze and can't remember her newest married name. Then I do. "Hello, Mrs. Wallace. This is Mary Jane."

"Okay."

I'm getting the feeling she just woke up. "Um . . . is Alicia home yet?"

"She's getting in tomorrow," she answers.

I'm stunned. "Are you sure? I thought she was coming today."

"Tomorrow." Her tone makes it clear that we're done debating the point.

"Well, thanks." I almost ask her to have Alicia call me when she gets in. But it wouldn't do any good. In all the years Alicia and I have been friends, her mother successfully relayed exactly one message. And that one came too late to do any good.

I hang up and dial Alicia's school number. This doesn't make any sense. Why wouldn't she come home today? And why wouldn't she call me? She had to know I'd be waiting for her.

"Hello?" She's answered on the first ring, but she doesn't sound any wider awake than her mother did.

"Alicia? How come you're still there?"

"I decided three nights in Attila would be about all I could handle."

"I was hoping we'd have time to talk tonight." I know I sound whiny, but I'm so disappointed, I can't help it.

No response.

"Why didn't you call?" I demand.

"Sor-ry. I just forgot."

I'm moving swiftly through disappointment straight into anger. "You forgot to call? When you knew I was waiting for you?"

"I'll be there tomorrow. And Friday. And Saturday."

I know she's probably staying the extra night so she and Colt can do . . . whatever it is they do. And I should be more understanding, especially since I know how she feels now. But the least she could have done was call me.

"Don't be mad, Mary Jane," she says. "I'll call you when I get in tomorrow. We'll have lots of time to talk. Okay? It'll be great."

She's saying the right words now, and I try not to feel like I feel. I don't want to ruin the little time she does spend here. "You're right," I finally agree. "It'll be great to catch up."

"So we'll talk tomorrow, okay?" This feels like an exit line to me, and I wonder if Colt's there with her right now.

"Okay. See you then, Alicia."

"Is Alicia coming over?" Mom asks when I join them downstairs.

"No. She's not driving home until tomorrow." I keep my voice light so she won't see how bummed I am.

Dad's home, too, now and has already gotten the fireplace roaring. He's standing over a giant bowl in the kitchen, tearing up pieces of bread for stuffing, while Mom and Sandy get boxes out of cupboards. "How's Alicia doing at school?" Dad asks.

"Good," I answer, although what would I know about it?

"Come on in!" Sandy shouts as if the three of them are in a swimming pool and I'm shivering on deck.

I wash my hands in the sink and start pulling lettuce, carrots, peppers, and cheese out of the fridge. On the night before Thanksgiving, we each know our appointed duties. I make my veggie and cheese salad that has to sit in the fridge overnight. Sandy stirs water into her bread mix, then dumps it into her bread loaf machine. Dad chops celery and gets the other ingredients ready for his famous Ettermeyer stuffing, which he'll prepare at dawn. And Mom pretty much does everything else.

"Who all's coming tomorrow?" I ask, checking out the twenty-four-pound turkey Mom has thawing in the fridge.

"Well," she begins, "there's us. And Uncle Jim. Grandma and Grandpa Ettermeyer left for Florida too early this year, or they'd be here. It's not going to be the same without them."

"We're making all this food for five people?" I'm pretty sure we could feed fifty.

"Ah," Dad says. "Five of us eat tomorrow, but four of us eat for months."

Mom snaps him with the dish towel.

It's true, though. We'll be eating turkey until Christmas anyway. And I really don't even like the stuff. Dark meat's too greasy, and white meat's too dry. I usually fill up on stuffing and potatoes. And Sandy's bread, of course, because she keeps track.

At least, keeping busy in the kitchen helps takes my mind off how mad I am at Alicia and how much I miss Jackson.

When I come downstairs on Thanksgiving morning, I can already smell the turkey in the oven.

"Marwyjan!" Sandy yells. "Come and see!" She sounds like she's been up for hours, in spite of the fact that she's still wearing her purple pajamas. Sandy is sitting on the floor in the living room, using the coffee table as her desk.

I peer over her shoulder as she presses her hand down on a piece of white construction paper and traces around her fingers. This is the worldwide trick for drawing turkeys on Thanksgiving, but it's not quite working for Sandy. The turkeys look pretty much like shaky hands, with varying numbers of finger-feathers. And every feather is, of course, purple.

"Wow! Turkeys! Great idea, Sandy!" I exclaim, picking up one placemat and admiring it.

"Turkeys for Thanksgiving!" she explains. "One for everybody eating."

"Another great idea." I ruffle her hair and join the kitchen crew, where I peel potatoes until I'm released for my shower.

Alicia doesn't call.

Jackson does. He wishes me Happy Thanksgiving and starts to say something romantic, but his grandmother says she needs the phone, and he has to hang up without saying he loves me.

But he does.

Turns out there are six of us, instead of five, for dinner. Uncle Jim bravely brings a date, although he didn't even bother to tell my mom. Dad is quick to point this out to his little brother as soon as they're alone in the hall. I take Uncle Jim's coat, so I get to hear the first of the sibling squabbles of the day.

"Are you ever going to get married, Jim?" Dad asks.

Uncle Jim shrugs and winks at me. "Too busy making money. And living the good life." He spreads out his arms to Sandy and me. "So where are my hugs?"

Sandy and I hug Uncle Jim. His suit feels like silk. But what I try not to stare at is his head, which is miraculously covered with hair after a decade of hairlessness. I can only imagine the kind of restraint it takes for my dad not to comment on this new addition to his brother's head. This is not a cheap rug or anything. I'm sure my uncle has purchased the most expensive hair money can buy, plant, or plug. So you might not even notice if you didn't know Uncle Jim in the *before* mode.

I watch as Sandy frowns at Uncle Jim's head. I'm waiting for her to say something about it, but she doesn't.

Uncle Jim's date joins us when Mom's through taking her coat.

"This is Rena, my executive secretary," Uncle Jim announces as if she's a gift to us.

Rena is wearing a silk evening dress that makes Mom, Sandy, and me look like bag ladies by comparison. I try to smile at her without laughing, but it's not easy. When Alicia's second stepfather was having an affair with his executive secretary, we used to call her the Ex Secs.

"Sandy," I say, leaving before I crack up, "let's make another placemat."

When we're all seated at the table, where Mom has quickly and discreetly added a sixth place setting, Uncle Jim reaches for the mashed potatoes.

Mom stops him. "Just a minute, Jim. We haven't expressed our thanks, and it *is* Thanksgiving." She turns to Dad, appointing him Sayer-of-Grace. "Honey?"

"Can I do it?" Sandy raises her hand like she's in school.

"Sure!" Dad exclaims. I think he's relieved. "You go right ahead, Sandy."

I catch a condescending look exchanged between Uncle Jim and his Ex Secs, but they bow their heads like the rest of us.

"Hi, God," Sandy begins. Nobody on earth prays like Sandy, although I've always imagined everybody in heaven does. My whole life I've loved eavesdropping on her chats with God. I used to volunteer to put her to bed at night—no small ritual—just so I could hear her prayers.

"Aren't you happy that everybody's taking today off to tell you thanks for everything?" she continues. "I guess we should do this every day, huh? Because we had food yesterday, too." Her words become clearer as she prays. "This is good food we're about to eat, maybe especially the bread. So thanks for making the stuff that goes into all of this food. Like that water and the white powder in my box of bread that makes it bread. And we're sorry about that turkey who had to die for dinner."

I peek around the table. Even the Ex Secs is smiling, and it's not a making-fun-of smile either. Sandy's eyes are the only ones wide open, as if she's talking to somebody sitting at the table with us, instead of somebody you have to close your eyes to see.

"Thank you for basketball and M&M's and my pillow and

that red bird on the window at breakfast and for breakfast and for Mommy's kiss on my forehead and Daddy's hug, the one that isn't too short or the one that isn't too tight, and for Uncle Jim having all of his hair back and for his pretty friend having a pretty dress, even though it isn't purple, and for Marwyjan's stories where I get to name the horses Apple and Betty and Wally and Goldie and—"

"Thank you, Sandy," Mom says. "We all have lots to be thankful for. Amen."

Inside my head, the voices have soaked up the Sandy-ness, and they're telling me I should be as thankful as my sister.

M.J.: *You should be thankful for this body that's healthy, with great sexy potential. And thankful for Jackson!*

Plain Jane: *You should be very thankful for your parents and your sister and this roof over your head, not to mention all of this food, when people in India are starving.*

But don't eat too much. You can't afford to put on weight, especially not before tomorrow night.

25

Alicia at Last

We eat too much and talk too much, especially Uncle Jim. His cell goes off half a dozen times during dinner, and Dad tries to make him turn it off. They get into it a little bit when Uncle Jim tries to give Dad advice on the stock market. Dad comes dangerously close to making fun of Uncle Jim's new hair when he asks if he's using hair gel these days. But they don't argue as much as usual, and Mom's good at changing the subject at just the right time.

After dinner, Dad and Uncle Jim and Ex Secs watch football games while Mom and Sandy and I wash a million dishes. Ah . . . those Thanksgiving traditions.

The phone rings.

I drop the dish I'm wiping, which, luckily, is plastic. "I'll get it!" I'm not sure if I'm thinking it could be Alicia or Jackson. I'll take either one, though.

I pick up the receiver and step out of the kitchen before saying hello.

"Mary Jane?"

"Jackson! Come home!" I plead.

"Wish I could. I've got thirty-two relatives here, and they're all serious Bellevue candidates. Can't believe I ever swam in the same gene pool as these people. I miss you, babe." He says this low, sexy, and it makes me tingle, which is a stupid word, but there it is.

"I miss you, too," I say, low and sexy, going for the same tingly reaction.

In the background I hear someone yelling for Jackson to come and eat.

"I'm going to have to go," he says. "Are we all set for tomorrow?"

"You bet," I say. I haven't cleared it yet, but I don't think there'll be a problem. Lots of times I go out with friends after Sandy's games.

"Well, Happy Thanksgiving," he says. "I can't wait to see you, Mary Jane. It's all that's keeping me going here."

When I hang up, I want to go directly to Alicia's and talk out everything. I'm dying to call and see if she's home. But I won't do it. She said she'd call me. I'll just have to wait.

Hours later, when the kitchen's back in order, the Ex Secs is flipping through magazines, and the menfolk are still watching football, I can't stand it anymore, and I dial Alicia's number.

“Hello?” It’s Alicia, and she’s answered on the first ring.

“You’re home!” I don’t add, *Thanks a lot for letting me know.*

“Oh. Mary Jane.” She actually sounds disappointed. “Hey.”

“Yeah. Hey.”

“So,” she says, breaking the silence, “what’s up? You have a good meal?”

“Fantastic!” I exclaim, hoping she’ll be sorry she didn’t get in on it. “You?”

“We’re not eating until later. Ed’s kids are coming.”

I soften a little because I know she can’t stand her current stepbrothers. They only show up once or twice a year, but it’s always a free-for-all. “That’s rough. So when are you guys escaping and coming over here?” I can’t imagine that she and Colt would want to spend quality time with her stepbrothers.

“I can’t get away for a while.” She doesn’t sound that upset about it.

“Well,” I continue, “Sandy’s been bugging me all day, wondering when you’ll be here.” It’s true that Sandy’s asked about Alicia. She really misses her.

“Tell her I’ll be over later.”

We don’t say much else, and when I hang up, I’m flooded with things I should have said, like “What’s the big idea? You’re acting like you don’t even want to talk to me!” And “You’re being a crummy, rotten friend, just when I need to talk to you the most.”

Maybe it’s good I don’t say everything in my head after all.

*   *   *

Another hour passes. Then another. I made the mistake of telling Sandy that Alicia and her boyfriend are coming over, so now she asks me every five minutes where Alicia is.

Finally, the doorbell rings. Sandy runs to answer it. When she sees Alicia, she lunges at her and almost knocks her down. "'Licia! 'Licia!" she cries, hugging her. Sandy's four inches taller than Alicia, so I can't see Alicia until they stop hugging. I don't see Colt anywhere.

"Is Colt coming?" I ask, peering out at the driveway.

She shakes her head. She's wearing jeans and a red sweatshirt and looks thinner than when I saw her last. Her hair is short, short, and it makes her eyes pop out. But that might be related to the fact that she's wearing so much makeup. She really does look college.

"Better come on in," I say, holding the door open. "Mom will yell at us for—"

"—letting in winter," Alicia finishes. She's heard my mom say this a million times. "You look good, Mary Jane." She walks in and hugs Sandy one more time. "And you look terrific, Big Sister!"

Sandy giggles and won't let go of Alicia's hand. "Where's your boyfriend?"

"He couldn't make it," she says.

I'm not sure if she means he couldn't make it to our house or to Alicia's.

She shrugs over at me. "He had to go to his house. His mom threw a fit."

Secretly I'm glad, because I think it will make it easier for Alicia and me to talk. But I feel guilty for thinking this. I couldn't stand it if I had to be away from Jackson that long. "That's whack," I say. "Sorry."

"Yeah. Well."

Mom comes out. "Alicia! It's so good to see you!" She gives Alicia a hug, so now I'm the only one who hasn't hugged her. "Can I get you something to eat?" Mom asks.

Alicia grabs her stomach. "Absolutely negative. But thanks, Mrs. Ettermeyer. It's good to see you, too."

Dad leaves the game long enough to come over and say "Hi" and ask Alicia about school, but Sandy's looking restless. She bounces from one foot to the other, still holding on to Alicia's hand.

"Cards!" Sandy shouts. "Want to play cards?"

"Are you kidding?" Alicia says. "Why else do you think I came over here?"

I love the way Alicia is with my sister, but the comment cuts a little. She sure isn't acting like she's here on my account, even though she knows how much I want to talk to her.

But Sandy is so excited that I shove my feelings to the back of my brain. Alicia and I will have plenty of time to talk after Sandy goes to bed, especially since she won't have to hurry back to Colt. "Let's play cards," I agree.

Sandy leads us to her room, where we sit at a small card table. The three of us have played at least a hundred million hands of cards at this table. Sandy's won every game.

"So," Alicia says, scratching her chin like she's trying to think of something, "what should we play?"

Sandy pulls out a deck of purple cards with white cats on them. "Go Sandy!" she suggests.

"My favorite game," Alicia agrees. "I forget. How many cards do we get in this game?"

"Duh," Sandy says. "Eight."

She proceeds to give herself ten cards, Alicia fourteen, and me six. "Pass three cards," she commands.

We obey. Sandy passes one. And the game goes on, as only "Go Sandy" can.

"So how's school really going?" I ask.

"Not bad, except for algebra."

"Is it really hard?"

"I'm not going to pass it."

I'm not sure what to say. Alicia and I never got As, but we never got Fs either. "What happened? What are you going to do?" I'm thinking it's a scary way to start a career at the university.

On command, Alicia gives Sandy all her black cards. "I got a little distracted."

"I hear that," I say, wishing we could talk about our mutual "distractions."

"First thing I told the rents as I walked in the door was that their little girl is failing math."

"Did your mom go postal on you?" I ask.

"She would have, except for a little thing called 'freshman forgiveness.'"

"Give me all your cards with cats on them," Sandy requests. Then she laughs her head off as we hand over every single card we're holding.

"So what's freshman forgiveness?" I ask.

"Your first semester, you can fail a course, ask for freshman forgiveness, and they wipe it off your record. It's like you never took the class, never failed."

"Sweet! Like a grown-up version of do-overs, huh?" I'm thinking this is a concept I'd like to see sweep the nation.

Sandy carefully sets down all of the cards, arranging them meticulously in no particular order I can make out. "I win!"

Alicia fingers the cards and screws up her face. "Rats! You did win. And here I thought I might have a chance at last." She stands up from the table. "What time's your game tomorrow, Sandy?"

"Seventy-eleven," she answers, without a moment's hesitation. Time in Sandy's world is always either seventy-eleven or thirty-fourteen.

I stand and stretch, too. The chairs in Sandy's room are the same size they were in elementary school days, when we fit into them. "Translated into Illinois Standard Time, that would be four-thirty," I clarify.

"Great. I'll see you guys at Roy Dale." She moves toward the door.

"What?" She can't possibly be leaving. She's barely been here an hour, and we haven't even talked about Colt or Jackson.

"I gotta jet," she says.

Sandy doesn't protest, but she slumps in her chair and stops gathering cards.

"I thought we could talk, Alicia. You could stay all night, since Colt's not here."

She shakes her head. "I'm really tired."

"But I need to talk!"

"I'm not leaving town or anything. We can talk tomorrow." She waves to Sandy. "Can't wait to see you play, kid. Go, Dragons!" And she walks away.

I feel like punching her in the face. But all I see is her back as she leaves Sandy's room. She's supposed to be my best friend. I can't believe she's doing this.

I run after her and catch her in the entry as she's slipping into her jacket. "Alicia, why are you acting like this?"

She frowns. "Acting like what?"

"Like you don't want to be here? Like you don't care that I need to talk to you? Like . . . like a jerk!"

"Excuse me?" She looks smug, superior. "Who's acting like a jerk?"

"Both of us!" I shout. I see Dad and Uncle Jim and Ex Secs staring over at us, so I lower my voice. "Listen. I have to talk to you about Jackson."

She rolls her eyes. "Don't get all high school on me, Ettermeyer."

I stiffen. That one hurt.

"We'll talk later. Okay?" She says this like I'm five and she's promising to take me out for an ice cream. "Just not tonight." She walks out, leaving the front door open and winter pouring in.

26

The Main Event

Friday morning I get my hair done (it looks great), my nails done (they feel great), and I shop at Victoria's Secret (not too racy, but nothing my mother would wear either). The shopping spree takes longer than I expect, but it gives me empathy for what Robbie and Pretzel Boss must be going through at the mall on THE day.

Part of me feels like Christmas, thinking about being with Jackson tonight. Another part of me is scared for the same reason. And another part is sad, thinking about Alicia. Plus, the voices in my head are at it again:

Plain Jane: *Why did you have your hair styled like this? It's too fancy.*

M.J.: *Your hair looks hot! You're sexy.*

Plain Jane: *Are you sure you want to do this with Jackson? I don't remember you making up your mind.*

M.J.: *True. You didn't actually make up your mind, but so what? Just let things happen. Tonight is the biggest night in your whole life.*

I ride to Sandy's big game with Mom and Dad just in case Jackson gets back in time and meets me there. Sandy's in the backseat with me. She's smiling like she doesn't feel an ounce of pressure.

As we turn a corner, I catch Sandy's profile. For a second I can't breathe. She looks old—her age anyway, nineteen. That's when I remember Chris and the mystery phone call.

"Hey, Sandy," I whisper.

Mom and Dad are safely occupied in a discussion about fixing the garage door that's started not staying down again. Their mature conversation is going something like: Dad: "I can fix it myself." Mom: "No, you can't." Dad: "Yes, I can."

Sandy turns and grins at me. "Yes, Marwyjan?"

"I was talking to Red at your last game."

"I like Red."

"She likes you. She says her brother Chris likes you, too."

Sandy nods. There's not a trace of embarrassment on her face. But she's not volunteering any information.

I press on. "Red says Chris called you."

"On the phone," Sandy elaborates.

"Yeah? Anyway, Red says Chris asked you if he could kiss you."

She grins a little bigger.

"So," I try, "did he? Did Chris ask if he could kiss you?"

She nods.

"What did you say?"

Her face scrunches up like she's trying to remember the exact words. "No, thank you, Chris." She smiles again.

"That's it?"

"Yep." She goes back to staring out the window as we cruise into the Roy Dale parking lot.

It's amazing how crowded Roy Dale gym is. The Richmond Raiders are here in full force. I wander all the way to the top of the bleachers instead of sitting with the rents. I fold my coat next to me, saving a seat in case the real Alicia shows up, the old Alicia I could talk to.

The game starts, and Sandy gets sent in after five minutes of play. I remember to yell, "Go, Dragons!" instead of "Go, Sandy!" I can hear my parents screaming the same thing from their post several yards over.

I can tell Sandy hears me. She turns and looks up into the stands, then grins when she spots me. Her gaze moves on, sweeping the bleachers, and I know she's looking for Alicia. I could wring Alicia's neck for not being here for my sister.

For the next few minutes, Sandy is more of an on-the-court spectator than a player. But she gets the ball a couple of times when it rolls right to her. Then she dribbles and passes it off, like it's too hot to hold. Watching my sister is such a kick that I forget about everything else for a while.

"Sweet! Sandy's in!" Alicia hands me my coat and plops next to me. She's not wearing any makeup today, except mascara, but she's sporting an SIU sweatshirt, just in case anybody would ever forget she's in college now. "How's she doing?"

"Okay." I turn back to the court. I don't want to say anything else to Alicia because everything I'm thinking about saying is filled with nastiness.

"Go, Sandy!" Alicia shouts.

"Don't yell that," I snap. "You know she wants us to cheer for the team and not just for her."

"Well, excuse me," she fires back. "Oh, I get it. You're all hurt because I'm late. Or is it because I didn't come home on Wednesday? Or that I left too early for you last night? It's hard to keep up with your personal injuries, Ettermeyer."

That hurts. But I'm not about to let her see it. "I don't care when you come or go, Alicia. Because you know what? You're not the Alicia I used to know."

"So that's it," she says in that same smug tone. "You're all upset because I've changed at college? Because I'm Colt's girlfriend and not high-school Alicia anymore?"

"Maybe you're right," I say evenly. "Maybe that *is* it. All I know is I don't like Colt's girlfriend very much."

I expect her to storm off, but she doesn't. I think about sitting somewhere else, but I was here first. And this is where Sandy will look for me if she wants to see me during the game.

I try to block Alicia out of my head, pretend she's not here, and just watch the game.

With only a minute left in the first half, Michelle sends Larry out. It's a total surprise move on our competitive coach's part, and I get the feeling she wants to get it over with while we have a decent lead.

Larry seems even more nervous than usual and stands farther out of bounds, closer to the bleachers than to the court.

The whistle blows, and the game goes on anyway. Sandy walks over to Larry, even though the other players are rushing to the far court. She's smiling at Larry, who rocks back and forth, holding his arms as if that's all that keeps him from falling apart.

When she's a foot from him, she stops. Then she holds out her hand. Larry stares at it. His arm moves toward hers, then slaps back into that self-hug. But Sandy keeps her hand where it is. And after one more false start, Larry reaches out and lets her take his hand in hers.

I don't think anyone in the bleachers is watching the game. The gym has turned silent. Everybody knows what's happening, what it means. Even the Richmond parents and fans, who've never seen Larry before, know, the way soldiers in battle know soldiers they've never met before because they're all part of the same struggle.

He takes a step, and she steps with him. Another step. And another. Until he's inbounds. And still Sandy leads him farther out onto the court. They move closer to the basket. They're almost to the free throw line. We're all on our feet.

The only sound in the gym is the *thump thump* of the basketball, the occasional squeak of a tennis shoe.

Then Sandy shouts to Chris, "Throw me the ball, Chris!"

Chris turns, and in that instant he must understand. He stops dribbling and throws Sandy the ball. She lets go of Larry's hand, catches the ball, and hands it to him.

Larry takes the ball. And as if his arms are on springs, they stretch out instantly, shooting the ball. It misses, but it hits the backboard hard, with a *bong!*

Larry took a shot, in a real game.

The whole place explodes in cheers. There's no score, but it's the biggest victory we've ever seen. The roar of the crowd is so loud that Larry covers his ears and rocks back and forth. But his face says it all. His eyes disappear in a huge smile I've never seen before.

The Dragon bench empties, and Larry's teammates circle him, jumping and clapping as the buzzer sounds the end of the first half. The kids know better than to hug him or pat him on the back. Even the Raiders have stopped a safe distance away to cheer.

Tears are streaming down my cheeks. I won't look at Alicia because I don't want her to make fun of me, of this.

Then I hear her. She's the only one in the whole gym sitting down. Her head is in her hands, and her shoulders are shaking.

And she's sobbing.

27

Voices

"*Alicia?" I sit down* beside her. I don't know what to do. I don't think I've ever seen her cry. Not even when she nearly sliced off her finger.

She cries harder, if that's possible.

I put my arm around her shoulders. "Alicia, what's wrong?" I think I'm scared. Alicia has always been the one who could keep things in perspective when I got out of control.

She looks up at me. Her face is covered with tears and snot. Mascara tracks her cheeks in long, dark streaks. "Colt didn't have to go home. His parents couldn't care less where he spends Thanksgiving. We just . . . we just haven't been getting along."

"You'll work it out," I say lamely, trying to make her stop crying. "Everybody has fights. You should have heard my rents in the car."

Alicia looks down at her hands. "I think he's going to dump me, Mary Jane. What if he breaks up with me?"

I stare at her in wonder, not at Alicia, but at myself. How could I not have seen this? "I—Alicia—I didn't know. I'm so sorry."

"I thought he was the one, Mary Jane. I still think he is . . . even if he doesn't." She glances up at me. "Isn't that pathetic?"

"No!" I want to say more, but I don't have a clue what I should say. "You love him."

"He said he loved me, too. But he couldn't have. Now he says he doesn't know how he feels or what he wants. I just got off the phone with him. How could he love me one day and then not the next?"

"It's not your fault," I say, searching for words. I haven't even met Colt, and I'm as close to hating him as I've ever come to hating anybody. "Maybe he's, like, disturbed. Or a con man. Whatever he is, you're too good for him, Alicia! The guy's obviously not who you thought he was."

"That's not what hurts the most," she says. "Maybe *I'm* not who *I* thought I was."

I can't think of anything to say to that.

"How could I have been so wrong about him? About *me*? I don't even know who I am anymore."

I want to help her, but I can't. I have no answer for her. But the voices in my head are talking, calmly, reasonably, like they always do at Roy Dale, when I'm around Sandy and her friends. The thoughts in my head aren't one voice, one note, but they fit together, like a chord. So I listen:

M.J.: *Alicia is a beautiful, intelligent college woman. She's the strongest, best friend you've ever had.*

Plain Jane: *Alicia is a dumped girlfriend, who gave this guy something she can't get back. She feels rejected, foolish, ugly.*

M.J.: *But she's not! She's sexy and confident. . . .*

Plain Jane: *And lonely and scared . . .*

And then I get it.

I'm not the only one with voices in my head. There must be at least a couple of Alicias fighting in her head—the confident college girl, Colt's girlfriend, Sandy's buddy, *my* best friend.

And what about Colt? Maybe part of him did love Alicia, *does* love her. And maybe another part of him just wanted to get her into bed.

What if everybody has voices? What if life isn't simple for anybody?

I feel as if I'm on the verge of an incredible discovery, an amazing secret of the universe. But I don't know how to explain all this to Alicia.

I reach over and hug her. "You'll be okay," I say.

"I don't know, Mary Jane. I don't know what to believe anymore."

I pull away so I can look into her eyes. The old Alicia's there. So is the new one. Maybe some I've never met.

"Hey! Don't cry." It's Sandy. She's left the game and is towering over us, her face screwed up like she might cry, too. "I don't care if we lose the game."

I glance at the scoreboard and see the Dragons are down by fourteen points. "Oh, honey," I say, taking her hand, "that's not why we're crying."

"But why? Why are you crying? Why's Alicia crying?" Sandy is really upset.

"I guess," I begin, trying to respect Sandy enough to be honest but struggling to put it into words she can understand. "I guess we're crying because we're mixed up." I glance over at Alicia. She's sniffling, but the crying's stopped. "And sometimes it feels like we're different people, like a bunch of Alicias live inside her head and a bunch of Mary Janes live inside mine."

Alicia's eyes narrow, and her face looks like a light's gone on inside. "That's exactly it," she whispers. She looks up at Sandy. "And sometimes it's hard to know which Alicia is real, which one I really am."

Sandy breaks into a smile that shows her crooked canines and too much gum. "That's easy!" she exclaims. "You're everybody! You're your whole team. And you're the captain!"

Sandy kisses the top of Alicia's head, then trots back down to the Dragon bench.

When she's gone, Alicia turns to me. "I'm really sorry, Ettermeyer. I was pretty scummy to you. I don't blame you if you hate me."

"Are you kidding? Haven't you ever heard of freshman forgiveness?" I ask. "It's sweeping the nation."

We talk off and on through the third quarter. She tells me about Colt. I tell her about Jackson. I think I feel more *me* than I have in a long time.

In the fourth period, Alicia elbows me and points to the Dragon bench. My sister has her head on Chris's shoulder, and his arm is around her. It only lasts a minute, but I think the image will be with me forever. Neither of us says a word, but I can tell Alicia feels what I feel. Sandy isn't just a little girl. She's also a nineteen-year-old woman. And maybe more. My sister is "the whole team," too.

When the game's over, and we cheer our 46 to 20 loss, Sandy comes over to make sure Alicia and I are all right. Her smile is even bigger than it was before.

"You're awfully smiley," Alicia observes. "How come?"

Sandy's face shows an angelic wonder. "I just feel really happy."

"Yeah? And why are you so happy?" I ask.

Sandy's eyes narrow, like she's thinking it over. She tilts her head to one side, and a shadow splits her face into two, dark and light. "I'm not sure," she begins slowly, "but I think it has something to do with Chris putting his arm around me." There's no joking in these words, not a bit of teasing, no guile. Just pure joy, as if she's as surprised as the next guy at this new development.

Alicia throws her arms around Sandy's neck and hugs her. "You know, kid, I want to be you when I grow up."

"Okay," Sandy says. Then she skips back to her team to celebrate.

My cell goes off. I check and see it's Jackson's number. "Hello?"

"Mary Jane, I tried to call you a couple of times," Jackson says. I hear the windshield wipers in the background. "Everything okay?"

"Yeah. Sorry. I didn't hear my cell. I'm still at Sandy's game. Lots of noise here."

"Cheering?"

"And crying." I smile at Alicia.

"Your team lost, I take it," Jackson ventures.

"Yes." I could try to explain to him that nobody here ever cries over a lost game, that we've been crying because it's not easy realizing how complicated everybody is, especially ourselves. But I don't know if he'd understand.

The thought hits hard. There's a lot he doesn't understand about me and a lot I don't understand about him. Too much. I've got Mary Janes he has no idea of. I wonder how many Jacksons there are that I haven't met.

"Well, I'm in town and headed to Roy Dale. Wait for me, okay?"

I wait for him outside, as the first snowfall of the year descends in giant flakes. The parking lot clears. I stare up into the sky, already black as night. I could be inside a snow globe, with white flecks swirling around me, sticking to my eye-lashes, tickling my ears. It's still, as if padded and sealed. I'm not sure I've ever felt this peaceful.

Jackson honks as he pulls up to the curb.

I get in, and before he can say anything, before I get thrown off guard by how amazing he looks and smells, I blurt it out. "Jackson, we have to change our plans."

"You're kidding! Why? What happened?"

"Nothing. I mean, I just can't do this."

"Mary Jane," he begins, his voice all full of niceness and sexiness, "you don't have to be afraid of anything. I'll—"

"It's not that," I interrupt, because it isn't. I'm not afraid, not like he's thinking. "I'm just not ready, and I'm thinking I probably won't be, not until I know someone well enough to marry him, and he knows me well enough to marry me back."

I've blindsided him, and I know it.

"I don't get it." He's been leaning close to me, and now he pulls back and sits up straight. "Why did you let me think we were going to be together tonight? You can't just change your mind like that. Without even telling me? This isn't right, Mary Jane. I've been good to you."

"What—so sex is a thank you?" I snap. "I *owe* you because you've been good to me?"

"I didn't mean it that way," he mutters. But he doesn't try to tell me how he did mean it.

"I know." I take a minute and struggle to get my words

out single file so they'll make sense. "Jackson, I'm sorry to spring it on you like this. But I couldn't tell you before because I only figured it out now, tonight."

Someone flashes his headlights behind us, then honks. I think it's the Roy Dale principal, and he doesn't like us loitering in his parking lot.

Jackson pulls away from the curb and out of the lot. "So can we at least talk about this?" he asks.

"I want to talk about it," I answer. I'd do just about anything to make him understand what's going on inside of me, why I've come to this decision, why I know it's the right thing.

But neither of us talks as he drives to his house. He pulls into the driveway and leaves the motor running.

"So talk," he says, like he's mostly mad at me.

I wait and listen to the voices in my head. Now that I understand them better, I want to hear them out. But I'm the one who'll make up my mind. I'm the captain.

"Jackson," I begin, prompted by ***M.J.***, "I want you so much! I won't lie to you. I wanted this night to happen as much as you did. I'll probably hate myself in the morning for not going in with you right now."

"So let's go in," he says, although I think he knows I won't.

I keep going, taking my cue from **Plain Jane** now. "You make me feel beautiful, Jackson. Did you know that? I don't think I've ever felt beautiful before. I still can't believe you chose *me.*"

"I *thought* we chose each other." He's sulking now.

"We did. We still do, I hope. I'm not saying I want to break up with you. And you better not want to break up with me just because I'm not having sex with you tonight. I love you more than any guy I've ever known, more than I thought I could love anybody. And I know there's so much more for me to love. I want to know you better and better. I just don't want to have sex. Okay, I do. But I don't. I'm going to wait, Jackson, because it's going to be worth it."

Jackson turns his big brown eyes on me. "I just wanted us to be together."

I keep talking as snowflakes curtain the windshield and our breath collects on the glass. I don't bring up the stuff about the vow and the cow. I don't tell him about my charter membership in AIA. But I translate these things into words I think he'll understand if he lets himself. About waiting, about saving.

It's weird. One minute Jackson acts like a little boy who didn't get the gift he wanted for Christmas. The next minute, he acts like the popular guy he is, giving off vibes that this is no big loss to him. And in the next minute, he seems to get it. He might even look relieved. I don't know, but I think I see the Jacksons in his head struggling, too.

"I better take you home," he says when we're both too exhausted to argue anymore.

We're quiet until he turns onto my street. "Not exactly the night I had planned," he observes.

"Tell me about it," I agree. "I've got sixty-seven dollars in Victoria's Secrets that shall remain a secret."

We grin at each other.

He stops in front of my house, and we exchange an awkward, nervous kiss, then say good-bye.

"I'll call you," he says.

I nod. I want to believe him. I want him to call me. I want this to end happily ever after, with Jackson vowing to wait, too, and to date only me for the rest of his life. I want to surround us with words like *together* and *forever.* But I don't know which Jackson will win.

I watch him drive away, his taillights turning circles of snow red and yellow, his tires leaving gray streaks in the white snow. I miss him already.

When I get inside the house, Alicia's sitting on the couch reading Sandy a book about unicorns. Mom and Dad are in the kitchen, pulling out leftovers for an after-hours snack.

"Everything okay?" Alicia asks.

Sandy's staring at me, too, waiting for my answer.

"Yeah. I'm okay." It's true and not true. Complicated, like everything else.

Mom hollers from the kitchen, "Cassie called. She wants you to call her back."

I plop on the couch with Alicia and Sandy and dial Cassie's number. Alicia goes back to the unicorn story, and I let Cassie tell me about a guy she met at the mall. Jessica and Samantha are in the background, and I hear them arguing about which DVD to put in.

I want to see them. I think I need to see them. "Why don't you guys come over? Alicia's here. And my rents are rounding up leftover turkey to munch on."

Cassie passes the invite to Jessica and Samantha, including the lure of the leftovers. They make gagging sounds at the suggestion of turkey sandwiches but say they'll be right over.

By the time they get here, we've started a game of "Go Sandy!" We move to the floor and circle in front of the fireplace.

"Can you teach us to play, Sandy?" Cassie asks.

Sandy gives each of my friends her killer smile and hands them a bunch of cards to share. "Your turn now," she says to Samantha.

Samantha glances at Jessica, as if asking for help. Jessica shrugs. So Samantha turns to Alicia.

"Looks like we've got some easy marks here, Sandy," Alicia says. "Some rookie card players. Let's show them how it's done."

Sandy complies by asking and receiving everybody's "boy cards," followed by their "girl cards." She sets them down in perfect couples.

It makes me think of Jackson. I wonder what he's doing now, if he's all alone in that house. If he's thinking of me. If he still loves me.

Alicia secretly squeezes my elbow. When I look at her, I know she's reading my mind. And I know she understands.

I made the right decision.

"Turkey sandwiches, anyone?" Dad shouts from the kitchen.

We burst out laughing. "Maybe later, Dad!" I shout back. "Thanks!"

"Give me all of your cards with kitties on them!" Sandy demands.

We peer at the backs of our cards, but there aren't any kitties there, just horses. Sandy looks, too, now, and she's not happy.

"Where are the cat cards, kiddo?" Alicia asks.

"I left them in the car!" Sandy looks as concerned as if she'd forgotten real kittens in the freezing car.

I hop up off the floor. "I'll get them."

I dash out to the car, retrieve Sandy's cat cards, and start back in. Snow covers the ground and continues to float down. I shuffle up the white-cushioned sidewalk under a quilt of stars. Christmas music is playing from the house across the street. Through the Ettermeyer picture window, I can see Alicia and Sandy by the fireside, surrounded by The Girls.

Again, I think of Jackson. With all my heart, I hope he'll call me. If he doesn't, I'm thinking ***M.J.*** may never speak to me again.

But I know that's not true. I'll be okay no matter what. And ***M.J.*** and ***Plain Jane*** won't stop speaking to me. I understand where they're coming from now. And as I stop at my door and gaze up at the snow-speckled blackness, I'm listening.